AN ACADEMIC DEATH

AN ACADEMIC DEATH

J. M. Gregson

This first world edition published in Great Britain 2001 by
SEVERN HOUSE PUBLISHERS LTD of
9–15 High Street, Sutton, Surrey SM1 1DF.
This first world edition published in the USA 2001 by
SEVERN HOUSE PUBLISHERS INC of
595 Madison Avenue, New York, N.Y. 10022.

British Library Cataloguing in Publication Data

Gregson, J. M. (James Michael)
   An academic death
   1. Lambert, Superintendent (Fictitious character) – Fiction
   2. Hook, Sergeant (Fictitious character) – Fiction
   3. Police – England – Gloucestershire – Fiction
   4. Detective and mystery stories
   I. Title
   823.9'14 [F]

ISBN 0-7278-5748-7

Typeset by Palimpsest Book Production Ltd.,
Polmont, Stirlingshire, Scotland.
Printed and bound in Great Britain by
MPG Books Ltd., Bodmin, Cornwall.

*To Michael and Christine,
who finally got married whilst
this was being written*

One

'I don't care if I never see the bastard again!'

The woman sat with her arms folded and her chin out, challenging the man on the other side of the desk to dispute her view.

Detective Sergeant Bert Hook studied her calmly, refusing to be hurried into any hasty response. She was no more than thirty-five, his experienced eye told him, running a little from the buxom to the squat. She had blue eyes and a shock of gold-blonde hair, which fell a little over her left eye with the vehemence of her assertion. She brushed it away impatiently, as if she feared that Hook would do something underhand whilst he was hidden from her full vision. Bert eventually said, 'Do you have any reason to think that your husband might be in trouble, Mrs Upson?'

'No. If he fell down the bog, he'd come up with a five-pound note, that one! He's always been a jammy bugger, Matt has.'

'Yet you thought you should come and tell us that he had gone.'

'Yes. Thought you were supposed to report a missing person, didn't I? Look, if you don't want to know, that's all right with me! I just wish I hadn't wasted my time coming in here!' She unfolded her arms and set them by her sides, gave him a more intense version of the glare he had become accustomed to since the desk sergeant had brought her into CID.

Yet she didn't stand up, didn't give any other sign of wanting to be on her way. Mrs Elizabeth Upson wanted

1

this desertion to be registered, he reckoned. Bert allowed a smile to spread slowly over his large, weather-beaten face. 'It's usual to report a missing person, yes. But you should know that if people are adults, we can't force them to return, not against their will. Of course, we can point out that they have family responsibilities and suchlike, but if they don't choose to come back and honour them there's nothing—'

'I don't want the bastard back! I thought I'd made that clear. I might refuse to have him, even if he came.'

Bert was playing his usual game of pretending to be obtuse. Many people had underestimated the intelligence behind that impassive, bovine face in the fourteen years he had spent in CID, and a large proportion of them had suffered in consequence. He was more interested at present in the attitude of this woman than in the routine details of the missing person she was reporting, and the impatience he was inducing in her was making her reveal more of herself than she had purposed when she came into the police station at Oldford.

He studied her impassively for a moment, watching the colour heightening in her cheeks, listening to her breathing as she strove to make it more even. Then he repeated with infuriating slowness the information he had already recorded on the pad in front of him. 'Matthew John Upson. Aged thirty-seven. Height five feet ten inches. Weight just over seventy-six kilograms.' He looked into the flushed face on the other side of the desk. 'That's your twelve stones, you see. We have to record weight in metric, now.'

'I'm well aware of metric measures, Sergeant Hook. I'd have given it to you in kilos, if you'd asked me at the time.'

'Good, good.' Her whole tone had changed once the anger overlaying her absent husband had been diverted. She was asserting now that despite the epithets she might choose for her absent husband, she was not to be lightly dismissed: this was an articulate, middle-class woman. But Hook took her back to the missing man. 'How long has he been missing, Mrs Upson?'

'Since last Friday morning. He went out of the house and never came back.'

'Four days, then. Three nights. Did he give any indication that he intended to go away for a time? Did he pack any clothes, for instance?'

'No. I've checked that. All the clothes except the ones he went out in are still in the house. So is his shaving kit.'

Intelligent and perspicacious, Mrs Upson, decided Bert. Probably she was telling the truth. If so, Upson hadn't intended to go. Or hadn't meant anyone to suspect what he was planning: the two could be very different. 'Did he appear distressed or agitated in the days before he disappeared, Mrs Upson?'

She sighed – an angry, petulant sigh rather than one of resignation. 'No more than usual. I'd have told you if he had.'

'I have to ask you this. Can you think of any reason why Mr Upson should have wanted to leave his home? On a permanent basis, I mean.'

She folded her arms again, accentuating the line of her substantial bust by the action. 'You mean did he have another woman lined up, don't you? Well, at least you're getting round to some proper questions at last, I suppose. The answer's no. He'd had a few flings over the years. I shouldn't think any of them would have been stupid enough to take him on.'

Nor he to set up another partnership, perhaps, if he thought the first attempt was a fair guide. A phrase about once bitten twice shy swam disconcertingly into Bert's mind in the face of this formidable female. He said instead, 'How would you describe your own relationship with your husband, Mrs Upson?'

She set herself, almost as if this was the question she had been waiting for, as if she were a markswoman aligning her sights. Then she said vigorously, 'He was an arsehole, Sergeant Hook. An arsehole, pure and simple!'

Bert resisted the line about arseholes, like the truth, being rarely pure and never simple. There was a time and a place for everything. He bent over his pad, recording that the home relationship was not happy. Mentally, he noted the more significant fact that she was already speaking of him as in the past. Shouldn't she have said, 'He's had a few flings over the years' rather than 'He'd had' and 'He *is* an arsehole rather than 'He was'? Aloud, he said, 'Thank you for being so frank. Can you think of anywhere where your husband might have gone?'

'No. That's why I'm here. He's not at his mother's. He's not at his sister's. I can't think where else he might have gone.'

'What about close friends?'

'He hasn't got any. Not any that would be stupid enough to take him in, anyway.'

Bert smiled the reassurance he normally offered in such cases. 'We'll add Mr Upson to our missing persons register. But you'll probably get a phone call or a postcard in the next few days. Then you'll wonder what all the fuss was about.'

Liz Upson stood up. 'No fuss, Sergeant. I just thought you ought to know he was gone. Thought I was supposed to register the fact. And for the record, I won't be pleased to hear from him. Arsehole I said, and Arsehole I meant.' She spoke the word with a capital letter, and it seemed to give her a peculiar satisfaction. It was as though she had lighted upon a succinct summary of her missing husband, and was determined to fix it in her memory by repetition.

'We'll need a recent photograph.'

She nodded, reached into her bag, produced a clear colour photograph, handed it across the desk. Bert Hook registered her beautifully manicured fingers with the CID man's automatic talent for detail, noted again the contrast between how carefully she had prepared herself for this visit and the immoderate language she had used about the missing man, and then looked down at the photograph. A man with dark, thick hair over a square face, staring directly at the camera with only the slightest of smiles beneath a long upper lip. It looked like an enlarged version of a passport photograph. 'This will do very nicely. If you hear anything of his whereabouts, please don't forget to let us know. People often do, in their relief.'

She looked at him contemptuously, and he thought there was going to be a renewed vituperation of the man in the photograph. But perhaps she realised belatedly that she had already told this man more about herself than she had planned, and she merely nodded curtly.

Hook guided her out through the labyrinth of Oldford CID. She strode back into the outside world without a backward glance, paused for a moment when the sun hit her face, seeming to relish the late-afternoon June warmth. She carried the air of a woman who had completed another task in a busy day. She moved well. Bert, who was built on generous lines himself and was of a charitable disposition, decided that Mrs Upson was buxom, after all, rather than plump. Her summer dress clung to all the right places. From the rear as well as the front, she was a shapely woman. And from this distance you could almost forget her bitter tongue, which seemed in any case to be confined to the subject of her husband. Bert stood in contemplation at the station entrance until she disappeared. It was a pity he wouldn't see much more of those ample curves.

But DS Hook had no idea how well he would get to know the formidable Mrs Upson in the weeks to come.

Two

M atthew John Upson was duly entered into the Oldford police files as a MISPA. Within hours, he was on the national computer lists as a missing person; moreover, he was recorded as a man who had disappeared without any apparent intention of doing so.

But in the Britain of the twenty-first century, many thousands of people disappear each year. The problem is one of numbers and police time. Unless there are suspicious circumstances about the disappearance or the person involved is a minor, it is an economic fact of police life that not much time can be given to searching for people who are suddenly absent from their previous residences. A few disappearances have tragic or sensational consequences, which are invariably well publicised and intriguing to the public – Lord Lucan has passed from the realms of popular curiosity into those of popular humour.

But most people who disappear have their own reasons for doing so. Only a tiny minority are criminals. The majority of the rest eventually resurface, though not necessarily in the same spot where they disappeared beneath the waves. There is not much point in devoting scarce resources to investigating these sudden absences.

Unless, that is, someone has reason to think there is something sinister about them.

Matthew Upson's disappearance had been reported by one woman and been dutifully entered into the files of bureaucracy. It was in the system, and there it might have remained undisturbed almost indefinitely if it had followed the usual pattern. But then, three days later, on Thursday the 17th of June, another woman came forward and protested that this particular disappearance did indeed have something about it which she thought highly suspicious.

The woman had a considerable presence. But police stations are used to those, and are more than usually proof against their impact. This lady's air of patrician command might not have carried her far without the accusations she brought with it. Matthew Upson's sudden disappearance might have some odd circumstances surrounding it, she maintained. It might even be, she contended, that there had been foul play involved in it.

The police machine is formidable, but not inflexible. The woman who carried these suspicions was Mrs Rosemary Upson, the mother of the missing man. And within twenty minutes of her arrival at Oldford police station she was ushered into the office of Superintendent John Lambert, head of the CID section, where her allegations might receive appropriately weighty consideration.

Lambert had a copy of the bald facts of the computer entry before him on his desk. He went through the details of the time and circumstances of the disappearance with his visitor, noting her air of determination and her increasing impatience as she confirmed them. Then he said, 'I believe you think there is something more that we should know about this matter, Mrs Upson.'

She looked into the long face, noting the lines of experience around the grey, observant eyes and the mouth with its slight smile of encouragement. She had heard of this man and his reputation in solving the serious crimes of the area: this was the man she had been determined she would see. She was slightly surprised that she had got into his office to see him without needing to be more fierce in her demands.

Rosemary Upson said quietly, 'I don't believe that Matthew has simply disappeared, Superintendent Lambert. I think something has happened to my son.'

She had thought that he would try to reassure her, that he

would mouth the platitudes she had heard from others and assure her that her son would turn up unhurt. Instead, he studied her for a moment and then said, 'Are you telling me that you think your son may be dead?'

'Yes. Just that.' She felt her skin tingling around the base of her neck as she said the words: it was the first time she had voiced the thought so baldly.

Again that brief interval when he studied her and weighed her words, forcing her to do the same. Then he said calmly, 'And why do you think that this might be so, Mrs Upson?'

She had expected to be challenged, even gently ridiculed. She had been prepared to shout at unresponsive faces, to thump desks if necessary. This calm acceptance was somehow more disturbing. She tried to organise her thoughts rationally. 'The way in which he disappeared. It was so – well, so sudden and unexpected.'

Lambert smiled at her. 'Lots of people choose to depart like that, Mrs Upson. They have a vast variety of reasons for doing it. Only in a tiny minority of cases have they died.'

It was the first gesture towards anything like comfort that he had offered her. But it emerged not as comfort but as an invitation to justify her fears. She said determinedly, 'I saw him the day before it happened. Last Thursday. I'd have known if he was planning to disappear of his own accord.'

'That depends upon what your son was planning and why. He might have needed to deceive you along with the rest, even if he didn't wish to do that.'

She smiled grimly. 'I am his mother, Mr Lambert. Have been for the last thirty-seven years. I'd have known.'

Such was the depth of her own certainty that Lambert found himself believing her, against all the inclinations of his own years of experience, of hearing such assertions from parents. He said, not unkindly, indeed with a quickening of interest, 'Is there anything you can offer me which is more than a mother's intuition?'

She could not believe how calm she was now. She was sitting here trying to convince a senior detective that her son was lying dead somewhere, yet she was coolly marshalling her thoughts, wondering how she might best persuade him. Some of her poise was coming, she was sure, from this calm, unemotional figure on the other side of the big desk, so obviously prepared to take her seriously, so ready to listen to her worst fears about her son.

She took a deep breath and said, 'Matthew and I have always been very close. I haven't approved of everything he's done over the last few years, I haven't liked some of the people he has associated with. I don't deny that he has taken to concealing some parts of his life from me. But that doesn't mean that we haven't remained very close, Superintendent. I'd have known if he was planning to disappear from my life, even temporarily. He wouldn't have wanted me worried. And even if I'm wrong about that, even if you think these are no more than a fond mother's ramblings, that he wouldn't have told me what he was planning, I assure you that I would have picked up something of his intentions, whether he had said anything openly or not.'

She finished this breathless, for she had poured it out swiftly, fearful of an interruption, apprehensive that he would point out the thinness of her arguments. Instead, he studied her for that now familiar instant of silence before he said, 'Let's be quite clear about this, Mrs Upson, because what you're saying has very serious implications. You believe that your son has not disappeared from his home and his work voluntarily; that some person or persons have removed him from the scene against his will, and for their own purposes.'

She nodded, thankful of the pause his words had afforded her to make her breathing more even. 'Exactly that. I'll go further. I very much fear that he has been permanently removed from the scene. I shall be surprised if he is found alive.' She listened to herself as she spoke, and was surprised how calm she sounded.

'You don't think it is possible that he is merely being held somewhere against his will?'

J. M. Gregson

She felt a curious kind of relief in his quiet questions. She had expected to be treated as a hysterical female, called upon to justify herself, soothed and sent away to recover her equilibrium. Yet he seemed to be not only taking her seriously but prepared to push things forward, perhaps to escalate the investigation of Matthew's disappearance. 'It's possible, I suppose. But I can't see why anyone would do that. No one's going to rescue my son with a ransom, so that couldn't be the motive. I think some people wish to silence him, and his permanent silence can only be secured in one way.'

Her voice, which had kept an unnatural calmness for so long, quavered on the last phrase, and she felt the first hot tears pressing round her eyeballs.

Lambert felt a surge of compassion he would not show for this woman of over seventy, proud, even patrician in her bearing, who had probably never set foot in a police station before, who had no doubt had to force herself to come here on this mission for her son. He said quietly, 'You'll need to give me some details of the people you feel might be dangerous to him, Mrs Upson. We'll treat them as confidential, of course. I only hope that you will prove to be way off-key in your thoughts about this.'

He gave her a smile which was meant to be encouraging, but it felt forced and mirthless, even to him. There was something about this woman which made him think she was not given to hysterical reactions, that she retained an objectivity even about those whom she loved. She said, 'That wife of his. Elizabeth. Liz, as she likes to be called.'

Lambert nodded, intervening before she could be too intemperate to remind her, 'It was Liz Upson who reported Matthew to us as a missing person.'

'Yes. After he'd been gone for four days. She rang me and told me. It was the first time I knew that anything was wrong.'

'You speak as if you are not very close to your daughter-in-law.'

10

She glanced at him sharply, as if she suspected irony. 'We've never got on. I don't feel I know her very well, even now, after all these years of the marriage. Matthew realised it was a mistake, of course, when it was too late. She was quite a beauty, you know, when he first knew her.' She offered the fact as if it might serve as an explanation for her son's blindness to other things.

'Do you think your daughter-in-law might be involved in any way in your son's disappearance?'

She looked full into the grey eyes and the long, serious face. 'I've thought about it. She might be, as an accessory. I think she'd had enough of Matthew, of the rows and the arguments. I'm not saying the faults were all on one side, you understand. I'm sure Matthew has given her cause enough for complaint, over the last few years.' She spoke the last sentence reluctantly, delivering the phrases without her previous flow, as though they came only because she was determined to be fair.

'Wouldn't a divorce have been much less dramatic?'

'Matthew didn't want one. He still thought he could patch things up with Liz. And there are two children, you know; he didn't want to lose them. Eight and ten they are, a boy and a girl.' For a moment the blue eyes of this formidable septuagenarian shone bright with a grandmother's pleasure and pride.

Lambert threw her back immediately into the harshness of her suspicions. 'Mrs Upson, I have to remind you that you are making a most serious accusation, even if it is not as yet against any specific person. You are suggesting, to put it at its bluntest, that your son might have been murdered. You must therefore be completely frank with me. Are there people other than his wife whom you think might have had some hand in his sudden disappearance?'

It was her turn to pause, to weigh the consequences of this situation she had been so determined to create for herself. The bright, intelligent blue eyes stared for a moment into the observant grey ones of the man on the other side of the desk. Then she said reluctantly, 'I can't give you names. Matthew has associated with some pretty doubtful people over the last few years. I told him what I thought about the way his life was going, but I didn't want to know the detail of it. But I've no doubt if you investigate his disappearance, you'll turn over some stones and find some pretty unsavoury creatures underneath them.'

Lambert smiled grimly. 'You may well be right. The resources we assemble for a murder investigation throw up all sorts of associations. But let me be as frank with you as I think you have been with me, Mrs Upson. We can't begin such an investigation without a body, or at least without more tangible grounds for suspicion than you have been able to offer me thus far. At present, your son is no more than what the police call a MISPA, one of the many thousands of people in this country who go missing each year, for an infinite number of reasons. The vast majority of them eventually turn up unhurt, and I hope that your son may be one of that majority.'

'So do I, Superintendent. I have never hoped more strongly in my life that I might be wrong about something. But your statistics do not convince me: I am still sure that something has happened to Matthew.'

Lambert regarded her gravely. There was still something about this doughty woman in her mid-seventies that convinced him, despite the flimsiness of the evidence she brought with her to support her thesis. He said, 'I'm not saying I shan't be treating what you have brought to me this afternoon seriously. But we have to proceed with caution. I shall institute some discreet enquiries, beginning among my own officers. If we think there are grounds for suspicion, we won't let matters rest until we have some answers. I shall report any findings to you in due course. Meantime, if you find anything to support your fears – or, more happily, something which might allay them – please let me or someone else in the CID section here know immediately.'

He stood up. Mrs Upson rose, stiff but erect, and shook

his hand. 'I shall certainly do that. Thank you for listening to me, Mr Lambert. I pray God these have been no more than an old woman's wanderings. But I have a feeling that neither you nor I believe that.'

At eight o'clock on a perfect June evening, Superintendent Lambert and Detective Sergeant Hook were off duty and wandering among leafy glades. Most people would have said they were relaxing after the cares of the working day, but Bert Hook would have disputed that. For they were playing golf.

And Bert, who had come to the game late and reluctantly, contended that you could never be completely relaxed on a golf course. He maintained steadfastly that golf was the most stupid of games, though it now had him securely in its clutches. After twenty years of fearsome pace bowling and late-order big hitting on the cricket fields of Herefordshire and Gloucestershire, Bert Hook had thought that any game where you approached a dead ball and hit it in your own time must be an effete charade, unworthy of his attention.

He was still trying to demonstrate this. Usually the most mild-mannered of men, Bert now yelled, 'Come out of there, you bastard!' after his unhearing ball as it disappeared comprehensively into the trees to the right of the fourth.

Lambert allowed himself the superior smile of the single-figure player. 'Fairly tight driving hole, this,' he said unnecessarily, after he had despatched his controlled slice over the rise and on to the invisible fairway.

'Too bloody tight,' growled Hook. They didn't speak again until they met on the green, several shots later.

Lambert looked across to May Hill, with its knoll of trees on the summit looking surprisingly close in the still evening light. 'Nice course, Ross-on-Wye,' he observed contentedly.

'But the fairways are too bloody tight!' repeated Hook. 'Don't know why I joined this club. Don't know why I persist with this stupid bloody game!'

Yet even as he spoke, he knew that this wasn't true. He was glad he had been lured into this game he could go on playing as long as he could walk round the course, felt privileged to be walking these rich green and almost deserted acres on an evening like this. He would just have to get better. Then he would enjoy it more. He smote a surprisingly straight drive down the long fifth and was gratified to find it fifteen yards in front of John Lambert's effort. That would keep the smug bugger in his place.

Bert, who would have defended his chief to the death against station gossip and the envy rank brings with it, found Lambert sometimes insufferably patronising on the golf course. But he was beginning to realise that his feelings varied a little with how they both happened to be playing.

It was not until they were returning towards May Hill up the long sixth that Lambert said, 'It was you who saw Matthew Upson's wife when she came in to report him as a MISPA, wasn't it?'

'Yes. Strange woman. Came in to report he was missing, and started by telling me she hoped she'd never see him again!'

'Hmm. His mother came to see me this afternoon. She thinks something's happened to him. That her son hasn't just made off with another woman or fled from his debts. But she's no real evidence to offer in support of that.'

Bert thinned the 4-iron he had chosen for his second and hurled a lurid oath after it. Then he said, 'The wife was bedworthy. What you'd have called buxom, she was.' He allowed himself a low animal growl of appreciation as he recalled the retreating contours of Mrs Liz Upson.

'But you say she didn't get on with her husband?'

'She said he was an arsehole, to be precise. Quite early on, she said that. And she added other words, all equally unsavoury. But I got the impression that that wasn't her normal vocabulary. She was quite well spoken, otherwise. Well dressed, well made-up.'

'But she did come in to report he was missing.'

'Not until he'd been gone for four days, she didn't.' Bert played his ball from the rough near the out-of-bounds fence on the right and succeeded in concealing his surprise when it bounced appealingly on to the green. 'Rather gave me the impression she was just covering herself against future events, the buxom Mrs Upson did.'

Lambert ignored what he considered his opponent's good luck. 'We have to allow for the fact that old Mrs Upson who came in to see me this afternoon is a mother, naturally anxious about her missing son. But she didn't strike me as a panicker. I think we should look into this a bit, not just keep Matthew Upson upon the MISPA register.'

Which just goes to show that quite sensible decisions can occasionally be taken on a golf course.

Three

The Malvern Hills are Herefordshire's most striking physical feature. On a map, they make no great impression: they are no more than nine miles long, and the Welsh mountains not far to the west of them are much higher and hugely more extensive.

Yet the Malverns are more significant and command more affection than their size would suggest. They were a source of inspiration to the nation's greatest composer, Edward Elgar. They are set between two of the realm's ancient cathedral cities, Hereford and Worcester, and the lands stretching away from their feet witnessed some stirring battles in the nation's civil wars of the fifteenth and seventeenth centuries.

Moreover, they rise almost sheer from the fertile plain of the Severn and the picturesque town of Malvern below them, so that they appear both grander and taller than they are, and offer splendid perspectives in all directions, over at least ten counties. The Worcestershire Beacon, which is their highest point, is no more than 1,395 feet high, and there is even a paved path snaking along the spine of the ridge towards it. Certainly there is not here the remote grandeur or the airy magnificence of the great mountains of the Lake District or the Scottish Highlands.

But the Malverns are accessible to all but the seriously aged and infirm, being surrounded by roads and crossed by a honeycomb of paths, and they well repay the modest effort involved in walking them. The old can pant a little, take their time, recall the climbs of youth, and assure themselves that there is life in ageing limbs for a few more years yet. And the young are safe here: the slopes are ideal for children. And with sheep not usually in evidence, the Malverns are a wonderful playground for dogs.

On the longest day of the year, 21 June, when their primary school day was over, three boys and a dog took a picnic and cans of gassy mineral water to the sun-kissed western slopes of the Malverns. The eldest of the boys, Thomas, was eleven and the youngest eight, and the eleven-year-old took his leadership duties very seriously. Thomas insisted on going first along the track, and he supervised the smallest boy diligently upwards across the gently rising ground, though that sturdy climber gave every sign of having the greatest energy of the three. It was Thomas who yelled a series of futile commands at the black Labrador cross-breed, which had long since learned to ignore his shrill insistence.

It was Thomas who determined that they should walk some way between the head-high bracken and the trees on the lower slopes of the hill before they fell upon their picnics, which would otherwise scarcely have travelled half a mile from home before being consumed. They felt no need to climb to the very top of the hill: such goals were part of the impenetrable world of adults. They found a secluded spot halfway up its slopes, off the path and in the shade of a mountain ash.

Thomas became more officious. He urged his two juniors not to bolt their food, not to feed the persuasive dog, to wait for their drink of pop until they had finished eating. The youngsters ignored him for the most part, but they found that his commands echoed the admonitions of their absent parents, and were thus curiously reassuring.

The boys lay for a while on their backs, peering through narrowed eyes at the blaze of the sun through the waving seed heads of tall grasses. They knew that this was what you did when you were replete after a picnic: they had seen people do it on the telly. But as they were boys, this interval between action lasted for scarcely ninety seconds. Then all three of them were active again in this private world they had discovered, and Thomas was trying to dictate what games they would play.

Resentment in his juniors welled into a physical challenge, and Thomas and his brother rolled in a trial of strength which was only half playful. It might indeed have become serious had the dog not joined in, with a joyful barking and a frenzied licking of faces which was quite indiscriminate. The two boys fell apart in red-faced laughter and fruitless instructions to their pet to cease his attentions.

With only three boys and a dog, there was really only one game which was possible, as the golden afternoon turned into evening and fatigue crept into the minds and bodies of even these hyperactive young beings: hide and seek. Their activities resolved themselves into a sporadic and rambling game, creeping ever lower down the side of the hill, interrupted pleasantly by diversions such as huge furry caterpillars and the sighting of a bright green woodpecker in the dappled shade of a copse of birch.

Unconsciously, they were making for home and the end of this long Monday. Though there were plentiful hiding places among the bracken and the bushes in this area where no paths ran, no one preserved his disappearance for long, because the dog, unaware of the rules in this strangest of human pastimes, would discover the hider and reveal his whereabouts with a delighted barking, amidst futile recriminations from his quarry and delighted laughter from the searchers.

They were not far from the road and the short journey home when the dog made another find. This time his barking rose to a new pitch of excitement and a more rapid frequency. 'Here, boy! Come, boy!' called Thomas, with a belated attempt to re-establish his leadership. The dog did not come. Instead, the urgency of his barking increased, as if he was summoning them rather than being summoned.

They were tired now, and each of them called in turn to the dog to come, rather than pursuing him into the under-growth. His excitement only increased; his barking grew into a crescendo.

It was Thomas who eventually decided that the eldest had better go to fetch him. With a muttered grumble, he set off towards their invisible but voluble pet. The dog half-crouched beside his find, bristling with excitement, uncertain yet what the reaction to this would be, but certain that it must be of interest. He looked from Thomas to the thing beneath the bracken and back again, but his barking never ceased.

Curiosity was stronger than exhaustion, and the two younger boys trailed wearily after Thomas towards the source of the canine commotion. They found that Thomas had turned to stone as he stood above the excited black dog and its discovery. But their arrival stirred him into slow-motion activity. Conscious of his senior status and the responsibility he bore to protect his siblings, he raised his left arm towards shoulder height, to prevent them from approaching nearer to the thing beneath the gently swaying fronds of the bracken.

They had no inclination to do so.

The face stared upwards and unseeing towards the sky above the undergrowth. Or rather it would have done, if its eyes had been still undamaged within their sockets. Bluebottles buzzed gently around the mouth and ears, as if anxious to protect their trophy from this human intervention. They rose for a moment as he stooped towards the face, then settled again around the small, neat hole in the temple, where blood and something else unimaginable had oozed forth and been consumed.

Thomas had stilled them all with the raising of his arm, but it was the youngest boy who broke their silence and forced the tableau into movement. His long, piercing scream of high-pitched terror sounded scarcely human, and caused the other two to start with their own horror. Without a word or a glance at each other, they seized a hand each and bore their brother and themselves away from the sight. This time the dog, sensing that they would not return, gave a last gruff bark over his discovery and then trotted quietly behind them.

Matthew John Upson had been transformed from missing person into corpse. Into a victim of foul play. Dispatched from this life by person or persons unknown.

Four

Detective Sergeant Hook glanced covertly at the woman in his passenger seat as he drove towards the mortuary. Liz Upson was carefully made-up and wore a navy blouse and a dark skirt. Her plentiful fair hair was carefully in place, drawn back over her temples, and her pale face was as inscrutable as a Buddha's.

Bert wondered if she realised that he had volunteered to drive her to the identification specifically to study her reactions. He decided after a few minutes that she probably sensed quite clearly why he was beside her. She remained perfectly composed throughout the three-mile journey to the mortuary. Neither of them spoke a word.

He parked carefully, twenty yards from the door which led to the small reception area, then paused for a moment before he got out of the car. 'It's not an easy thing to do, the identification of a body. But it has to be done by someone: the law demands it.'

'And I'm the nearest relative. No matter how far we'd grown apart, the law says that I'm the person to do this.' She afforded herself a grim little smile, perhaps in appreciation of the irony of that thought.

The mortuary assistant, John Binns, glanced at the detective sergeant speculatively as he brought the bereaved wife into the comfortably furnished but slightly clinical reception area. They were old acquaintances, Bert Hook and he, and Binns knew that there might be something significant in the sergeant's attendance here, rather than that of the police-woman he would have expected.

20

He took down the details of Mrs Elizabeth Upson and her relationship to the deceased in a studiously controlled and neutral way. You mustn't upset a wife who had come here to conduct the grim ritual of identification. But the mortuary attendant was only human, with human curiosity like anyone else. He had seen the corpse himself, knew that this was no death from natural causes. There was an excitement for him about this body. Murder. The word brought its hint of melodrama even to those who dealt every day with death and its consequences.

As he completed the details of the official form, Binns looked up into the pale, studiously unrevealing face of the woman on the other side of his desk. 'All we shall need from you after the identification is a signature to confirm that the body you are about to see is in fact that of your husband. If indeed you are certain that it is, of course.' Despite himself, what he had intended as a reassuring smile emerged as something very near a nervous giggle. Binns was better at dealing with bodies than with living people.

It didn't appear to disturb Liz Upson. She nodded curtly. 'I understand.' She had looked neither man in the face throughout the proceedings. Beneath the skilfully applied make-up her face had an abstracted air, like one concentrating on a job which must be done and fearful that if that concentration lapsed she might give away more of herself than she thought was politic.

Or was this too fanciful? wondered Hook. Was she merely a wife about to face a moment of immense strain, determined to get through it without an emotional collapse?

Binns led them to the door of the identification room, then paused awkwardly. He had done it many times before, but it didn't make the moment when he had to warn people to be prepared for a damaged corpse any easier to handle. He said awkwardly, 'You must be prepared for something of a shock, Mrs Upson. Your husband – if indeed it is he – will not be as you remember him. The body was outside for some days before it was discovered and there has been – well, certain damage to the face.'

'Yes. I've already been warned about that.'

'Would you like a moment or two to prepare yourself?'

'No. I'd like to get this over. As quickly as possible, and with a minimum of fuss.'

Binns nodded, led her inside with Hook a discreet distance behind her, and drew the sheet back carefully to reveal the damaged head.

From behind, Hook saw the shoulders lift beneath the navy blue blouse, heard the sharp intake of breath which had lifted them. They had cleaned up the mortal remains of Matthew Upson as well as they could for inspection. The eyes were shut upon the vacant sockets beneath; only the ragged, bloodless scratches on those lids hinted at the ravages the crows had wrought here. The gun-shot wound at the temple was on the far side of the head as the bereaved wife looked down upon it, but visible enough.

After her initial gasp, she gave no other sign of weakness. Instead, she stood very still for a moment, staring down at what she had been brought here to see. Then she said quietly, 'That's him. That's Matt.'

Binns got her sitting down as quickly as possible when she left the chill of the identification chamber. They were likely to faint on you without warning, these wives. This one didn't. She reached for the official form, signed her name in the space waiting for it at the bottom, and refused a cup of tea. 'I'll be on my way now. I'm sure Sergeant Hook has more pressing matters to attend to.'

Liz Upson was almost as silent in the car on the homeward journey as she had been on her way to the identification, answering Hook's attempts to prompt her into revealing her thoughts only with a series of monosyllables. She was at the door of her detached suburban house before she said, 'I won't pretend I'm going to grieve too long over Matt, after what I said to you about him last week. But it's still a shock seeing him like that, even when you're prepared for it.'

It was the first conventional thought Bert Hook had heard from her in two lengthy encounters.

Superintendent John Lambert sat in his office and pondered on where to start his probing into the life of the man who had just been translated from missing person into suspicious death.

That neat wound in the temple had been from a bullet fired at close quarters; that much was already clear. They would have to wait for the post-mortem report for a more accurate assessment of exactly how close the gun had been held to that damaged head. He was already guessing from the absence of a weapon at the scene where the body had been found that this man had not died by his own hand.

It was safer to assume that, from his point of view. From the looks of the body, this man had been dead for some time before his corpse was found. The statistics hammering in his head told him that most of the murders which were not solved in the first week of an investigation remained permanently unsolved; the clock was already running.

The routine machinery had already clicked automatically into action. The house-to-house enquiries around the base of the Malvern Hills were already being conducted with painstaking thoroughness. The team appropriate to a murder hunt was already in place.

It was time to start an urgent reconstruction of the life of Matthew John Upson, with particular attention to the last months of it, and minute attention to the final days and hours. Lambert had discovered the man so far only through the inevitably biased eyes of his remarkable mother. Normally the first step after the death would have been to interview that enigmatic wife, who had reported him missing a week ago and been so remarkably frank in conveying her dislike of her spouse to the phlegmatic Hook. She had already been with Hook to identify the remains and would no doubt be expecting a CID visit at any moment.

Lambert, who hated confinement within the four walls

J. M. Gregson

of his office even more than the paperwork which steadily accrued for him there, decided to let the amazingly candid Liz Upson stew in her own juice for a little while. If she had anything she wished to hide from him, her nervousness could only increase with the waiting. He decided to take Bert Hook with him to the place where the late Matthew Upson had worked for the last six years of his life.

Gloucestershire University was not an ancient foundation with ivy-clad elevations and obscure traditions. It bore as little relation to the dreaming spires of Oxford, fifty miles to the east, as its local football team, Cheltenham Town, did to Manchester United. Its status dated only from that curious period towards the end of the millennium when a Conservative government decided that almost any further education institution could call itself a university and a Socialist government had decided that the country should no longer provide grants for the vastly increased number of students.

The head of the department where Matthew Upson had worked seemed uneasy with his recent translation to Dean of the Faculty of Humanities. George Davies was a worried-looking man of fifty-six, with watery blue eyes and grey hair that had almost completed the process of recession from his domed forehead. Within a minute of opening a conversation with him, Lambert was wondering how much this bumbling man knew about his own staff.

'It's the administration, you see,' Davies said apologetically. 'It doesn't leave you time for much else. You always mean to get around the place and see what's going on, of course, but there's more stuff coming across your desk the whole time.'

'But you found Mr Upson an efficient member of your staff?'

'Oh, yes, I think so.' Dr Davies looked as if it was the first time he had given the matter much thought. His face brightened. 'Matthew had quite a good degree – Manchester, I think. One of the older-established universities in the north, anyway.' He smiled, then added nervously, 'Not that what we have to offer here isn't a perfectly acceptable product, of course. Definitely of degree standard, you know – whatever that is nowadays!' He laughed again, then looked embarrassed when he got no reaction from this senior policeman.

'So Mr Upson was a valued member of your team?'

'Oh, yes, I think I could say that. Never had a single complaint from a student about him, as far as I can remember.'

Lambert mused for a moment on this method of estimating staff. 'Did he have any enemies here that you are aware of?'

Davies was suddenly defensive. 'No. None at all. Superintendent, this isn't the kind of environment where people conduct feuds.'

'Nevertheless, we have a member of your staff lying dead in the mortuary with a bullet through his head,' said Lambert drily. He decided he had no more time to waste on this wooden figurehead. 'Dr Davies, I wonder if you could put us in touch with someone who worked closely with Matthew Upson on a daily basis.'

The hunted look left the ageing face. 'Yes, I'm sure I could. Let me see, Mr Upson taught Modern History – which means anything from 1485 onwards, you know!' He cackled at the thought; this was plainly a witty observation he had proffered on many previous occasions. He opened a prospectus on his desk and ran a finger down a list of staff. 'I think Charles Taggart might be your man. If he's around today, that is.' He pressed a button on his desk with every appearance of relief at the prospect of getting rid of his CID visitors.

His secretary took the CID men to the staff room, which had been relabelled the Senior Common Room when the institution had been designated a university. She explained on the way that not many of the teaching staff were around because the year-end examinations were in full spate. There was indeed only one person in the large room, whose oak panelling denoted the vanished elegance of an earlier era: this Georgian mansion, the administrative centre of the new university, was the one building of any age on the campus.

The figure gave no sign of registering their arrival in the room. Sandalled feet rested on an upright chair at the nearest point to them; then the eye was led over long legs in tight blue jeans, over a recumbent trunk and T-shirted torso, to a leather jacket draped over the shoulders and a floppy white sunhat, which was set upon the face so as to cover its every feature from the world around it.

The middle-aged secretary who had been their guide cast her eyes briefly to the stuccoed ceiling in silent disapproval, then indicated with a nod towards the supine figure at the other end of the room that this was indeed the man they had come here to consult. She made as if to depart, then looked approvingly at the well-pressed trousers and neat ties and shirts of the visitors. 'I can rustle you up a pot of tea when you've finished here, if you like,' she whispered.

Bert Hook thanked her, then shut the door carefully behind her as Lambert wandered down the long room with its pigeonholes and comfortable chairs to the recumbent occupant, who still gave no signs of registering their presence. He was standing very close to the invisible face as he said loudly, 'Charles Taggart, I presume?'

For a moment there was no reaction. Then a shudder ran through the long limbs and the hat was snatched away from what was revealed as a pale face with startlingly black and undisciplined eyebrows. Taggart sat up quickly, then held his head with a quiet groan. Then he scrambled to his feet and held out a large, strong hand. 'That's me. Except it's Charlie. Sorry, I had a heavy night last night. I was dozing it off, I'm afraid. What can I do for you?'

'You can tell us everything you know about a colleague of yours. Matthew Upson.'

The pale face fell. Taggart ran a quick hand over his heavy features, as if attempting to wipe away the after-effects of the previous night's debauch. 'In trouble, is he, Matt?'

'In the worst trouble of all, Mr Taggart. He's dead.'

Taggart's brown eyes widened. He looked from one to the other of his visitors, as if registering their appearance for the first time. 'You CID?' he said.

Lambert introduced himself and Hook. Then he asked, 'When did you last see Matthew Upson, Mr Taggart?'

Taggart frowned in concentration, then winced as his head hurt. 'A while ago. Sorry to be so vague. You lose track of people you see, once the examinations start and there's no teaching going on. A week? Ten days? I couldn't be sure. I saw him in here one morning at coffee time – spoke to him, in fact – but I'm damned if I can remember exactly when it was.'

'Did he seem agitated in any way?'

'No. No, not that I can remember. Look, if you're here investigating Matt's death, there must be – what do you call it, suspicious circumstances, mustn't there?'

Lambert gave him a mirthless smile. 'Highly suspicious. Matthew Upson was found with a bullet through his head.'

Taggart sat down suddenly, involuntarily. 'Bloody hell! Are you telling me that Matt blew his brains out? No wonder you wanted to know if he was – what did you say? – "agitated"!'

'I said that Mr Upson was found with a bullet through his head. I didn't say that he put it there himself, Mr Taggart. That's one of the things we're investigating. His body was only found last night.' Lambert and Hook sat down as though moved by the same strings. Four eyes studied the mobile features of the pale countenance that was no more than four feet away from them.

Charlie Taggart looked thoroughly shaken now. 'Sod me! Excuse me, Superintendent, but this has come as a hell of a shock, you see.' He ran a hand quickly through his mane of dark hair. 'Look, I think I can pinpoint the time I last saw him. It was immediately after I'd seen a problem student, a guy who hasn't put any course work in since Christmas, and I was sounding off to Matt about him. And it wasn't at coffee time. It was over a cup of tea on the Friday afternoon – about half-past three, it would be. I remember, because I asked him to go for a drink when we'd finished work for the week, but he said he couldn't.' He looked at the notebook which had mysteriously appeared in Hook's large hands. 'That's not last Friday, but the Friday before that.'

'Friday June the eleventh.' Hook entered the date and the time in his careful round hand as Taggart nodded. He looked up into the dark, deep-set eyes and said weightily, 'So far, you appear to be the person who last saw Matthew Upson alive, Mr Taggart.'

The statement had its effect. In these days of numerous real and fictional crime programmes on television, there are few people who are not aware that the last person known to have seen a murder victim alive is a source of lively interest, even suspicion, to police investigators. Charlie Taggart recoiled six inches on his seat, as if avoiding a physical blow. It was like softening a batsman up with a short-pitched ball, thought Bert, happily recalling his seam-bowling days.

But it was Lambert who followed up the tactic. 'You will appreciate that anything you can recall about Mr Upson on that afternoon may be vitally important. It is possible that he was dead within hours of leaving you.'

'Especially if it was me who killed him, you mean?' Taggart essayed a grim little laugh to underline how ridiculous that thought was. It was a mistake. Lambert's long, lined face did not crack into a smile; it merely studied him. Charlie ran his hand through his hair again in the short silence which followed.

'Did you kill him?'

'Of course I didn't!'

'Then don't waste our time with the suggestion, please. We've a lot of lost time to make up on this case. Did Matthew Upson appear distressed in any way on that Friday afternoon?'

'No. No, I can't say that he seemed any different from his normal self.'

'Which was what? Open? Reserved? Talkative? Morose?

You'll appreciate we have to build up a picture of someone we never knew. We can only do that through the eyes of those who knew him and met him often.'

Charlie Taggart licked his lips. 'I'm beginning to appreciate it, yes. This is a new experience for me. Well, I'd say he was friendly and open at work. Popular with his colleagues – most of them, anyway. There is a certain amount of professional jealousy and rivalry in a place like this, you know.'

'Yes. I understand that academics are noted for it,' said Lambert drily. He didn't doubt that academics could be as petty as other people – intelligence is no defence against the foolishness of human nature – but he doubted if lecturers round a professor could be as unctuous and obvious as a gathering of inspectors round a chief constable. 'Do you know of any of his colleagues who had a particular dislike for Mr Upson?'

'No.' His negative was as firm as if he was shutting a book. 'I'm not a historian as Matt was, so I don't know of any immediate rivalries, you see. I'm a social scientist, myself.'

He said it without a trace of embarrassment, thought Hook. Bert, who had almost completed an Open University degree himself, had heard a lot of jokes about sociologists in his years of part-time study. But perhaps with so many new and even more dubious disciplines proliferating in these new universities, the pressure was off the social scientists now.

Lambert said, 'So as far as you know, he had no serious enemies among his colleagues; he was in fact quite popular. What about students?'

A swift grin, equally swiftly removed. 'Matt didn't have any problems there. He was a good lecturer and a popular tutor.'

He recited the bland phrases almost as if he was writing them in a reference, thought Lambert. Perhaps they were just as meaningless. 'Equally popular with males and females, was he?'

29

Charlie Taggart glanced at him sharply, made as if to declare a diplomatic ignorance, then thought better of it. He smiled a conspiratorial male smile. 'He was a lively lad, was Matt. Quite a man for the ladies, you know. Went down very well with the girls, his tutorials did. He was never short of a bit of highly desirable totty, wasn't Matt!'

Lambert's heart sank, not at the chauvinism, nor even at the out-of-date slang, but at the thought of trawling through a mass of highly charged adolescent passions in search of a murder motive. 'Do you know of any particular girl who was close to him at the time of his death?'

A tiny hesitation. 'No, I don't.'

Lambert let the pause stretch out into long, quiet seconds as they studied him. There was a grandfather clock at the other end of the old, low-ceilinged room and they could hear its slow tick as they waited. He said quietly, 'We haven't had the results of the post-mortem yet, but I think you can take it that you are part of a murder investigation, Mr Taggart. In these circumstances, I need hardly remind you that it is your duty to give us all the help you can. If you are aware of any close relationships which involved Matthew Upson at the time of his death, you must tell us about them. It is not you but we and our colleagues who must decide whether they are relevant to this case.'

Taggart nodded slowly, looking past them at the empty armchairs on the other side of the comfortable room. He said dully, 'There was Clare, of course.'

'Clare who?'

'Clare Booth.'

'A student?'

Charlie smiled. 'No. A colleague here. She teaches economic history, I believe.'

No, thought Lambert, you don't believe, you know. You're trying to distance yourself a little from it, that's all. 'You'd better tell us everything you know about this.'

Charlie nodded his acceptance of that, then sighed heavily. 'She was younger that Matt. She came here four years ago, I think. She and Matt had a thing going. A serious thing, for a while.'

'Is she married?' Already Lambert was thinking of the difficulties of questioning her, of arousing the suspicions of a cuckolded husband who might still be in blissful ignorance of his state.

'No. I think – well, I think she believed at one time that Matt was going to marry her.'

'But she was deceived in that?'

'I don't think Matt ever – look, you'll need to question her yourself about that, won't you?'

'Indeed we shall. But the looker-on often sees more of the game than those involved, when it comes to affairs of the heart, as I'm sure you'll agree.'

Taggart looked at them sharply, then said, 'I never spoke to Matt directly about it, but he never gave me the impression that he regarded Clare as long term. I'm – well, I'm not even sure they were still together at the time he disappeared.'

'Well, that is something we shall have to ascertain, as I'm sure you'll agree. Now, are you aware of any other close liaisons Mr Upson had been conducting, inside or outside the university?'

Charlie gave an involuntary grin at the word. He still hadn't got used to the institution they used to call 'Karno's College' being referred to seriously as a university. 'No. But I wasn't aware of all his activities, of course. We were friends, but not what I'd call close friends; I didn't share many of his confidences.'

Was there a disclaimer here, an attempt to distance himself from some part of the dead man's life which would reflect no credit on him? Lambert looked at Taggart unblinkingly for a moment, then switched his tack. 'You say you asked him to go for a drink with you on that Friday, but he told you he couldn't. Did he say why he couldn't?'

Charlie Taggart frowned his concentration as he tried to remember, as if he were anxious to convince these two large men who studied him so unnervingly that he appreciated the importance of the question, that he was giving it due care and attention. 'He didn't say. Or if he did, I can't remember, which probably means it was something trivial. I know he was going to see this problem student, Jamie Lawson, just after we'd spoken, but that wouldn't have taken him long, so we could still have gone for a drink.'

Lambert stood up, then paused, as if struck by a sudden thought. It was an old ploy of his: when a person relaxed, thinking that an interview was at an end, he was often at his most unguarded. 'What would you say was the state of Matthew Upson's marriage, Mr Taggart?'

'I'd say not very good.' Taggart was immediately and noticeably guarded. 'But I can't give you any details. Matt didn't talk about it a lot, and his wife wasn't one for coming into the college much – or the university, as I suppose I should say now.'

Bert Hook looked up from his notes. 'You needn't think you're breaking any confidences. It was Mrs Upson who reported her husband missing a week ago. She didn't make any bones about her dislike for him. She said she wouldn't care if she didn't see him again.' He leaned his experienced face a little closer to the younger and paler one opposite him. 'As a matter of fact, she described him repeatedly as "an arsehole".'

Charlie smiled involuntarily. 'That sounds like Liz! Not one for mincing her words, when it came to Matt and his failings! All right, I knew that their marriage wasn't all it might be. You're saying that Liz thought it was considerably worse than that – that it was as good as over, in fact. I can't say that that surprises me.'

Lambert said, 'People aren't always agreed on these things. Do you think Matthew Upson was as resigned to the view that his marriage was finished as his wife?'

'I don't know. We didn't speak of it. I told you, we weren't bosom pals. I wouldn't have talked to him about the state of his marriage unless he'd raised the subject himself.'

'Which he didn't.'

'No. Not that I can recall, anyway. I didn't expect to be trying to remember the details of fairly casual conversations for the benefit of the law.'

It was a sentiment they heard all too often, and a fair enough protestation. Yet Taggart had been ready enough to recognise the attitude of a wife he scarcely knew, while asserting that he had learned nothing from a man he saw nearly every day. But sometimes people you saw but rarely left an abiding impression. Perhaps Liz Upson's forthright attitude had impressed itself upon Charlie Taggart as firmly as upon Bert Hook.

They reminded him once again that it was his duty to tell them of anything, however apparently insignificant it might be, which might have a bearing on the death of Matthew Upson, but he said he could not help them any more. If he saw any reaction among students or staff which might offer a pointer, he would get in touch with Oldford CID as suggested.

Charlie Taggart stood at the window of the deserted Senior Common Room and watched the police vehicle ease out of the car park and down the tree-lined drive to the exit of the campus. It hadn't been too bad. They hadn't pressed him hard in the areas where he had thought they might. He watched the brake lights come on as the car paused briefly before turning back into the road and the real world outside this academic island.

With a bit of luck, that might be the last he saw of the police.

Five

Liz Upson didn't normally drink alone, but she decided that this night must be an exception. Once the children were safely in bed, she poured herself a stiff gin and tonic, installed herself in her favourite armchair, and prepared to sip it slowly while she reviewed the tensions of the day.

Taken as a whole, it had not been as bad as she had expected. Identifying the body had been a bad moment, but she had always known that it would be. The headmistress had been full of understanding and sympathy when she had gone into the school to talk about the children and how they would react. The head had been divorced herself in the previous year, and Liz had eventually talked to her quite frankly about the state of her marriage with Matt at the time of his disappearance. She was surprised how much of a relief that had been.

They had agreed that unless the children were totally devastated by the news of their father's death they were better at school; following an established routine would itself provide a kind of therapy. Their form teachers would keep a special eye on them and report back on any reactions which seemed significant.

The worst part had been breaking the news of the death to the children when they came home from school. Yet even that had been worse in the anticipation than in the execution. They had not seen a lot of their father in these last two troubled years. There had been a few tears from both, some surprisingly percipient questions from ten-year-old Beth about how they would carry on without their father's earnings, some

34

snippets of reminiscence from eight-year-old Mark about football on the lawn and a visit to a pantomime.

Such good things would go on, she assured them, as she took them both into her arms. They would pull together and get through this. All her clichés of consolation came new-minted to them, so that they seemed to be comforted. It was much easier than she had thought it would be. Perhaps their father's disappearance and the inference she had drawn for them that he was not going to be around much in the future had prepared the way for this death, so that it came to them only as the brutal but logical culmination of a process which had started eleven days earlier.

She had done a thing she had not done for at least a year and read them a chapter of a favourite book, whilst they sat one on each side of her on the sofa in their pyjamas. They had been wide-eyed, earnest, concentrating hard on Harry Potter and his escapades, to the exclusion of their own situation. She had looked into their rooms an hour after they had gone to bed and found each of them sound asleep, with that unlined serenity in rest which only children's faces can show.

She realised as she sat in the chair how tired she was; tension brings its own exhaustion. And yet the day seemed curiously incomplete. She could not for the moment think why.

The phone shrilled suddenly at her elbow and she started from her reverie. It was the call she had expected. She gave her news, told the tale of the children's acceptance of their father's death, accepted the sympathy about the awful moment when she had seen Mark's damaged face at the mortuary.

'It was bad, but I didn't let it get to me,' she said. 'I got through it much better than I'd feared I would. . . . No, that stolid police sergeant drove me there, the one I saw when I reported Matt missing last week. . . . Well, we didn't say much, scarcely anything in fact. But he didn't seem to be suspicious. . . . I need to see you . . . No, I know, but— . . . Well, let's make it as soon as we can, eh? . . . No, they

haven't, but I'm sure they will. Of course I'll be careful –
if it's just that lumpish sergeant who went with me today, I
can handle him. . . . Yes, I suppose so. . . . I love you and
need you, darling. . . . Goodnight, my love.'

She sat very still in her chair after she had put down the
phone. She found herself suddenly very wide awake. And
she knew now what it was that had been missing from this
eventful day. No one from the CID had yet been here to
question her about Matt's death.

Lambert awoke with the dawn chorus, thought about the day
to come, and dozed only fitfully in the following hours. He
had that pain again, down the left side of his chest, not
agonising, but sharp enough to make him clench his teeth
with the pain. He held his hand against it, felt the pulsing
of the muscle from his heart, tried hard to convince himself
this was nothing serious.

By seven thirty he was wandering among his roses, removing the occasional dead head, savouring the scents as the
sun burned away the summer dew from his lawn and a
blackbird watched his every movement with eyes as bright
as polished beads. The pain was still there, but less sharp
now. He tried to forget it: he had enough problems without
hypochondria.

Christine watched him through the window of the bungalow and knew from his body language, from his abstracted air
even in the garden he loved, that he was fretting about a case.
Probably it was that lecturer who had been found with a bullet
through his head on Monday night in the Malverns. Where
once she would have been resentful that he was bringing
the horrors of his job even into this peaceful place, she
now felt only a protective sympathy for that tall, slightly
stooped figure, with the lined face and the still plentiful but
increasingly grizzled hair.

She brought him in and insisted he had some breakfast. She
even bore his ritual protests about the absence of the bacon
and egg and fried bread he claimed to miss so much. She

pretended not to notice how anxious he was to be away to face the challenge that death always brought into his life.

It was surprising how thirty years of marriage turned resentment into a sort of irritated love.

At eight thirty, Lambert was pacing restlessly round the Murder Room set up at Oldford CID, watching DI Christopher Rushton collating the information that was accruing from house-to-house and other enquiries. One of the problems with a body discovered so long after death was that no one could as yet be precise about the time of that death. The last recorded sighting of Matthew Upson seemed so far to be Charlie Taggart's casual encounter in the university Senior Common Room on the Friday afternoon of his disappearance. But it was still early days, and the uniformed men assigned to the task were having difficulty collecting information from Upson's students, since the normal teaching timetable had been suspended for the year-end examinations.

John Lambert was a dinosaur among modern superinten-dents, in that he refused to direct a murder investigation from behind a desk. He preferred to be out interviewing and assessing suspects, allowing Rushton to organise the information and the filing on the computer he loved back at Oldford police station. And Lambert could not stand this period of what he called 'the phoney war', where, in a case without an obvious suspect, the investigating officers had to wait for leads. He quizzed DS Hook about the wife in the case, and almost bit Bert's head off when he reserved his position on that enigmatic woman.

By nine thirty, he could stand the waiting no longer. He was assured in response to his urgent phone call that the post-mortem report would be typed and delivered to him by the end of the day, but he snapped that hours could be vital with a victim who had already been dead for so long, and strode out to his ageing Vauxhall Senator and a journey to see the pathologist.

His old acquaintance Cyril Burgess, MB, Ch.B., sat him down in an armchair in his office and had coffee served in fine china, as if they had all the time in the world to chat. Burgess had a taste for detective fiction as well as a propensity for quoting poetry, and he was delighted to have the break from the dull routine of corpse dismemberment which was afforded him by a suspicious death.

'Good clean death, this one,' he said cheerfully. 'Good clean corpse it would have been, too, if you'd got it to me a week earlier.'

'I apologise for the omission, but I can't take personal responsibility for it,' said Lambert drily.

'Late thirties, probably not a manual worker, by the state of his hands,' said Burgess.

'Sorry to disappoint you, but we know exactly who he is: Matthew John Upson, aged thirty-seven, Lecturer in Modern History at the new University of Gloucestershire.' Lambert bit with satisfaction into a ginger biscuit as Burgess's face fell with the dismissal of his detective flourishes.

'Well, at least he didn't have his head blown away with a shotgun. Not much skull left for me to examine, on that one you sent in last month.' It had been a family murder, with a son shooting a brutal father after a dispute on a farm and an arrest within three hours, but Burgess spoke as if he held Lambert personally responsible for the messy state of the corpse.

'He'll get away with manslaughter if he gets the right lawyer,' said Lambert impatiently. 'Tell me about Mr Upson, please.'

Burgess licked his lips. 'He was killed with a .22 bullet. I have the little chap right here.' He picked up a flattened piece of metal from a small labelled box on his desk with a pair of tweezers, looking at that moment like the consultant surgeon he might have been, if he had not preferred the certainties of dead bodies to the uncertainties of live tissue. 'It entered the head at the right temple and lodged in the skull, conveniently for us, whose job is to find who put it there.'

Lambert noticed that he had now allied himself with the forces of detection. He wouldn't cavil at that, if it made the pathologist more helpful. 'Did Upson put it there himself?'

Burgess beamed his delight. 'No. You can forget suicide, in my opinion. Your man was shot with a pistol, at close quarters – he'd have to be, for a .22 bullet to kill him, and to be fired with this accuracy. I'd say it was discharged from no more than a foot. There were clear powder burns around the wound. Probably more like three to six inches, if you want an opinion rather than the safe margins I'll have to specify in my official report.'

'Thank you. But in that case, why shouldn't he have done it himself?'

'Because he'd have had to be a double-jointed contortionist to hold the gun at the angle from which the shot was fired. The bullet entered his head at the right temple and very nearly emerged through the left forehead. It was almost certainly fired by someone standing behind him, who raised a pistol and cold-bloodedly dispatched an unsuspecting victim.'

'Unsuspecting?'

'He'd have turned, wouldn't he, if he'd known? Thrown up a hand maybe, or ducked. He certainly wouldn't have been shot from that angle if he'd known what was happening. I'm prepared to put that in my report and stand by it in the coroner's court, if it should be necessary.'

Lambert nodded. 'We didn't find a firearm anywhere near the body.'

'Ah! Murder, by person or persons unknown, then. The plot thickens. The spine begins to tingle!' Cyril Burgess gave his impression of a man with a tingling spine. The shiver went oddly with his immaculate dark blue suit and silk tie. 'A pistol. A derringer, say, or a Beretta. Light and attractive enough to appeal to a woman. Some femme fatale from the Riviera, perhaps, who will be left a million in his recently amended will!'

'You're stuck in the nineteen-thirties, Cyril. And the fictional nineteen-thirties, at that. Anyway, I don't see a university lecturer having a million to leave to anyone.'

'Academic intrigue, then! The Death of a Don.' Burgess

spoke the words like a headline; his relish was if anything increased. 'If only Dorothy L. Sayers was around to report your solving of the crime, you'd become a national celebrity, John.' Burgess gazed into the middle distance and shook his head sadly.

Lambert didn't think that the university he had visited on the previous day had much in common with the Oxford colleges of Harriet Vane, nor this murder much similarity with the puzzles she had explored with Lord Peter Wimsey. He said tersely, 'The corpse you have just cut up was discovered in the Malvern Hills. There is nothing as yet to connect the death with this so-called university where the man worked.'

Burgess shook his head sadly. 'Beware academic snobbery, John. Still, I don't suppose they have gaudy nights or college feasts in the new University of Gloucestershire: they wouldn't have the cellars for such things. Nor can they even manage a decent murder on the back stairs at dead of night, it seems.' He sighed heavily and turned his attention back to the real and less perfect world. 'Your man was in excellent health. All major organs in good condition. No reason why he shouldn't have made his three score years and ten and gone on after that. Except that someone chose to put a bullet into his brain!' The last thought seemed to restore his normal bonhomie.

Lambert thought how strange it was that the men and women who cut up corpses for a living should, in his now considerable experience, be habitually cheerful about their trade. 'I suppose you're going to tell me that he was killed somewhere else and dumped in the bracken at the bottom of the Malverns. The place where he was found is within seventy yards of a quiet road.'

Burgess shook his head. 'You have too melodramatic an imagination, John. I've always said so. You must stick to the facts, you know.'

Lambert said through clenched teeth, 'And the facts are?'

'Well, *one* of the facts is that he was almost certainly killed where he was found. There is no bruising on arms and legs which would indicate that he was lugged about immediately after death and delivered from a van at dead of night by heavily hooded figures, though I know that your taste for Gothic horror would welcome such a picture. I think he fell where he was shot and died immediately.'

'When?'

'Ah! There you pose a question which may be difficult, nay impossible, to answer with complete accuracy.'

'You can't help us?' Lambert made as if to stand up, knowing that Cyril Burgess would not lightly relinquish his contact with a juicy murder.

'I didn't say that, did I? I merely said I couldn't offer complete accuracy. When did he disappear?'

'On Friday the eleventh of June. The last sighting of him so far recorded is almost exactly eleven days before he was found on Monday evening.'

Burgess frowned thoughtfully. 'Eleven days and ten nights, to be strictly accurate. I'd say he died very shortly after your last sighting. In my opinion, that cadaver in there had been dead for around ten days when those lads found it on Monday evening.' He smiled happily at his audience of one, with the air of a magician who had just produced a large rabbit from a small hat.

Lambert stared at him. The time of death was a key thing in any investigation, and he had anticipated great difficulties in establishing it with a corpse which had lain undiscovered for an indefinite period. 'How certain are you of that?'

'Not certain enough to swear to it in court. Not yet. Call it informed opinion, if you like. It's the maggots, you see. Interesting little chaps, maggots.'

'They look well fed, then?'

'Yes. I'll show you if you like,' said Burgess, making as if to move out into the area where Lambert could still hear the faint sound of water running over stainless steel, washing away the detritus of corpse dismemberment.

The Superintendent held up a hasty hand, as Burgess had known he would.

'No use being squeamish about these things,' he said

41

cheerfully. 'Anyway, in this case you're lucky. We've only had the odd light shower in the period since he disappeared, and a high and fairly constant run of June temperatures. I've sent a sample of our wee maggot friends over to the forensic entomologist at Chepstow by special messenger, and I shall be surprised if he doesn't confirm my view.'

'Which is?'

'Your man had probably been dead for around ten days when I got at his remains yesterday. I'm expecting the expert at Chepstow to say between nine and twelve days, and you'd have to allow something like those margins for the report to be safe in court.'

Lambert nodded. 'And Upson was seen on the Friday afternoon of the day he disappeared. So we know that he was alive just a little over ten days before the body was found.'

Burgess was delighted to be allowed into the business of detection. He said triumphantly, 'So it looks as if he was killed within twenty-four hours of that moment. Quite possibly, on that same evening.'

Lambert nodded his satisfaction. It was the first real narrowing of the search he had been offered.

As he reached the door of Burgess's office, he paused and turned awkwardly towards his old acquaintance. 'I've had a bit of pain down the left-hand side of my chest lately, Cyril. Not likely to be anything serious, is it?'

Burgess managed somehow to follow a cheerful grin with a shake of the head which was quite grave. 'Too long since I was in medical practice for me to venture an opinion, John. Cadavers are my field, not living tissue. You can cut dead bodies up as much as you want, until you find the answer. Too much speculation for my liking, when you can't cut in deep and find out!' He looked at Lambert's torso as if he would have loved to cut deeply into it at that very moment. 'But you know as well as I do that chest pains might be serious. Better see your GP and have it checked out, hadn't you? Probably something o' nothing, but you can't take chances with tickers.'

His heart! John Lambert was sure it missed a beat with the mere suggestion that it might be damaged. He swallowed hard and said, 'I'll do that, then. It's probably no more than a touch of indigestion!'

But he knew that in thirty years of grabbing food whenever he could he had never suffered from indigestion.

It was almost midday now, but Liz Upson appeared cool, despite the summer heat. She stood looking at them for only an instant when she opened the door. Then, before Lambert could introduce himself, she said, 'You'd better come in,' and led Detective Sergeant Hook and the Superintendent into a comfortably furnished lounge.

The room was very tidy – surprisingly so, thought Hook, in view of the presence of two young children in the house. His own boisterous boys, the product of a late and happy marriage, rarely allowed a room to stay neat for longer than a few minutes. Patio doors gave a view of a long garden, a vista of neat grass with gracefully curving edges and the colour of blue hydrangeas and yellow and pink roses to attract the eye beyond the green.

The occupant of the property seemed as serene as the place itself. Liz Upson's abundant blonde hair was held back by a single band. She wore a full-length navy blue dress, which made her look slimmer than Bert remembered her from her visit to the station but still hinted as she moved at the curves beneath it. The navy leather of her shoes completed an outfit appropriate for mourning, but there was no trace of tears around the vigilant blue eyes.

Lambert said formally, 'I'm sorry we have to intrude upon you at a time like this, but you will understand that in the case of a suspicious death it is our duty to make certain enquiries as quickly as possible.'

She said firmly, 'I understand. I'm glad you came when the children were at school,' and they knew in that moment that she had been waiting for this, that she wanted to have the inevitable exchange over and done with. Nothing suspicious in that, thought Bert: the innocent as well as the guilty often feel like that, as they struggle back towards real life from the shock of sudden death.

But Mrs Upson had dressed carefully in dark clothes, and the curtains at the front of the house were drawn; was the woman who had insisted that her missing husband was 'an arsehole' now going to play the grieving widow? As if she were following his thought processes, Liz Upson added, 'There is no need to handle me with kid gloves, Superintendent. Sergeant Hook knows exactly what I thought of my husband.'

'I'm grateful for your frankness. Can you tell me, then, when you last saw your husband alive?'

He didn't stress the last word, and if she felt any implications in it, she chose to ignore them. 'Certainly. He left the house after breakfast on Friday the eleventh of June. So about half-past eight on that day.'

Lambert smiled. 'You are commendably precise.'

She gave him a small answering smile, and he became conscious that this woman might be an opponent worthy of his best efforts. 'It's information I have given before, when I reported Matt as what you called a missing person.'

'Yes. You left it until three and a half days after his disappearance to report him missing. Was that not rather a long time for an anxious wife?'

This time the smile was less fleeting, as if it was there to emphasise her confidence. 'It would have been, for an anxious wife, yes. But I was not anxious about him. As I indicated to Sergeant Hook at our meeting last week, I was not close to Matt.' Her blue eyes twinkled and her smile became dazzling as she turned it upon Bert's broad features, as if her scatological contempt for her husband on that occasion had become an amusing joke between them, and now a joke against herself with this death.

There are all kinds of reaction to the brutal business of murder, and Lambert was well aware that her lightness might be no more than a cloak for hysteria lurking beneath it. Nevertheless, he found her bearing an irritant: her calmness seemed to be wresting away an initiative that should be his in this questioning. He said, 'Are you saying that you weren't surprised when he didn't return on that Friday evening?'

She gave the question due consideration before she answered it, emphasising again how composed she was. 'Not unduly, no. I thought he might have given us a phone call, but it wasn't unusual for him to ignore such things.'

'"Us" being you and the children?'

'Yes. Who else?' She looked him steadily in the face, her blue eyes full of challenge.

'I've no idea. I trust you would tell me if there was anyone else involved.'

'Of course I would, Superintendent.' This time the smile definitely had an element of mockery. 'There was no one else here on that evening. You can check with the children if you like. But I hope you won't find it necessary to involve them.'

'So do I, Mrs Upson.'

'They'll miss their father for a while, but they'll get over it. He hasn't been around much for them in the last couple of years.'

'And why is that?'

She shrugged. 'You'll need to ask other people rather than me about that, I'm afraid. I'd lost interest in Matt's doings.'

'In your view the marriage was over.'

She thought for a moment again. 'In my view, it was. I wanted him out of the place. Out of my life, for good.'

'And now he is.'

It was a low blow, but she took it without complaint. 'Yes. And I'm glad of it. I told Sergeant Hook here as much, before it happened. I'm not going to indulge in hypocrisy, now that it has.'

'I'm sure that's highly commendable. There are other ways out of marriage than the death of a partner, however.'

She looked sharply into his eyes again, and for a moment Lambert hoped she was going to respond to his scarcely veiled insult. Anger, like other emotions, can be more revealing than calm. Instead she said, 'Divorce, you mean. Oh, I should have got round to it, in due course. But that bitch of a mother of his is a Roman Catholic, always going on about the indissolubility of the marriage bond. And Matt himself wouldn't agree to a divorce by mutual consent. He was frightened of losing his kids, he said. He'd have had access, of course, but that wasn't enough for him.'

Lambert switched his tack suddenly, hoping to catch her off guard. 'So where did you think he was on that weekend after he went missing, when you chose not to report his disappearance?'

She recognised the tactic and was not ruffled by it. 'With a woman, probably. Don't ask me to name one, I'd long since lost interest in his bedroom or any other activities.' For an instant, her contempt and loathing for the dead man sprang into her face with the words.

'But there were other women?'

'Yes. But I don't know or care who they were.'

For an instant, he was tempted to mention Clare Booth, the colleague at work with whom Charlie Taggart had said Upson had enjoyed a lasting relationship. But it might be more hurtful than she pretended. She had denied all knowledge of such associations, so she wasn't going to help him. Lambert sighed inwardly. If Upson had been a womaniser, as she implied, there would be a whole range of associations and intrigues to be unravelled in the search for his killer. Charlie Taggart had more or less confirmed that. He preferred monks to Casanovas as murder victims, any time, but there were precious few monks on offer.

He said abruptly, 'Did you kill your husband, Mrs Upson?'

For a moment, he thought she was about to laugh contemptuously in his face. Then she said, with the first hint of strain, 'No, I didn't. I suppose you had to ask, but you have your answer.'

'Then have you any idea who else might have put a bullet into his head? Think carefully before you answer, please.'

Beneath the dark silk, her bosom rose and fell sharply, but they knew it was anger rather than any softer emotion which moved her. Eventually she said evenly, 'No, I haven't. I'd tell you if I did. I wouldn't have wanted the father of my children to die like that, even if I no longer wished to live with him. I've thought furiously in the last twenty-four hours about who might have done this, as you might imagine, but I haven't come up with a single name. What I told you earlier is quite true: I haven't any clear idea of the people he has been associating with in the last two or three years.'

'Nevertheless, I shall ask you to go on thinking about the matter. If anything, however small, strikes you as odd, please get in touch with me or DI Rushton at Oldford CID immediately.' She nodded gravely. 'Did your husband possess a firearm, Mrs Upson?'

Again that sudden glance into his face; again the measuring of an opponent who might be worthy of her brain and her tongue; again the acknowledgement of a sudden switch of ground. She smiled, enjoying the surprise she thought her reply was going to give this grave, intelligent arm of the law. 'He did, yes. A pistol. I never handled it myself, and I wouldn't let him show it to the children.'

'Do you know the make of pistol?'

'No. I have no interest in such things.'

'Can you show us where he kept it?'

She hesitated for a moment, then nodded. 'I can, yes. I went through my husband's pockets yesterday, and found his desk keys.'

She led them through a spacious hall and into a small room which looked out on to the front garden. The curtains were drawn in here, in observance of the formalities of mourning that they had noted at the front of the house when they arrived, but she pulled the rope and swept them vigorously clear of the window. Sunlight flooded in, revealing a book-lined study and a wide mahogany desk with a green-leather top beneath the window. 'I've never been allowed to penetrate

# J. M. Gregson

the mysteries of his desk, but I know he kept the gun in the bottom right-hand drawer.'

She tried three of the various keys on the ring before she found the one which fitted, then, with a due sense of drama, slowly drew open the small drawer.

It was completely empty.

The lining of the drawer stared up at them like a mocking face. At Lambert's bidding, she unlocked the other drawers of the desk, but none contained the weapon. As she shut the last one, she said quietly, 'I suppose Matt must have taken it with him on that Friday morning. Perhaps he knew he was going to face some sort of danger.'

On that dark thought, they moved back into the hall, whilst she reiterated that she had no idea where the threat to her husband might have come from.

Liz Upson stood upon the step of the house for a moment after the detectives had got back into their car, watching them put on their seat belts and drive away, as if she wished to be assured that their presence had been removed from her world and that of her children before she shut the door on the world outside.

She made herself a sandwich for lunch and sat down with a pot of tea in front of the television and the one o'clock news. She didn't feel a need for anything stronger to drink, for the adrenaline of the interview was pulsing still through her veins. It was like her days of amateur dramatics in those far-off times before her marriage, when you had to wind down after a performance.

He was a shrewd bloke, that Lambert, she thought. Almost lived up to the press's reports of him. But she'd been a match for him. She'd almost enjoyed it, at times. She'd carried off the business of the gun pretty well. A useful diversionary tactic, that.

Six

The university halls of residence were almost deserted on this bright afternoon. Some students were sweating in examinations, some had finished and departed for the summer. Those who were left were either pursuing frenetic and belated revision in the libraries or seeking outdoor shade from the baking sun. Bert Hook thought longingly of the placid reaches of the Severn, lined with broad oaks, which were within a mile of here. Then he looked up at the high brick frontage of the four-storey building and followed Lambert through its entrance.

The man they had come to see was waiting for them in one of the chairs round the low tables which dotted the marble floor of the entrance area. It was the one large space in a building that was built primarily to house as many people as possible; despite its present deserted state, it was easy to envisage it as a meeting place, crowded with students drinking coffee, at the busier times of the academic year. Today, only the distant throb of pop music from somewhere above reminded them that there were some students still in residence.

The single figure in this broad space rose nervously as they came through the doors. 'You must be the CID people. I'm James Lawson,' he said. He held out a long-fingered hand as he came towards them, then decided abruptly that handshakes were not the thing for this occasion and thrust it awkwardly behind his back.

Lawson looked anxiously around him as Lambert introduced himself and his detective sergeant: the filth were not welcome in student culture, and he would not be popular for bringing them here. In the clichés of the young intelligentsia, the police were people who framed the weak and ignored or encouraged the criminally strong. He nodded absently as Lambert gave him their names, then added inconsequentially, 'Most people call me Jamie.'

Lambert said briskly, 'This shouldn't take very long,' and had a premonition even as he pronounced the words that he would not be correct.

James Lawson was slender, a trifle gangly. He wore the ubiquitous faded blue jeans which were the student uniform of the era. They were tight enough to emphasise his lean shanks and make his feet in their scuffed white trainers look larger than they were. His pale green T-shirt was old and had seen many washings, but it looked clean enough; it bore the name of a pop group of which Lambert had never heard. He was light skinned and fair haired, but his head had been shaved in the current fashion, and it was covered only with a very short yellow stubble; with his light blue eyes and the almost translucent skin on his cheekbones, he looked almost like an albino. Or someone who had been receiving chemotherapy for cancer, thought Hook, whose cousin had died of leukaemia in the previous year. People said the young could get away with anything, but fashion's dictates could expose them as cruelly as their elders.

'We can do this in your room if you think it would be more private,' said Lambert with a smile.

'No,' said Lawson, a little too quickly, so that the swift monosyllable immediately attracted the interest of these experienced men. But perhaps his room was just untidy, his bed unmade. He said, 'I'm up on the top floor. We'll go into the television room. We won't be disturbed there.'

He led them into a deserted room with a huge screen at the front and lines of well-worn chairs in front of it, some of which had upholstery bulging through slits in their covering. The room had been cleaned that day, so that none of the previous night's detritus remained. But the windows were shut and there was a smell of stale beer in the foetid room. There was another scent also which caught the nostrils of men, who recognised it immediately: the faint, sweet smell of cannabis.

Lawson glanced sideways at them, then walked over to tug at the cords and open one of the high windows, which were the only means of light and ventilation in this specialist room. 'I can't help you much, you know,' he said. 'It won't take long for me to tell you what I know.'

'Maybe not. But your tutor has been murdered, and you will understand that we need to get as clear a picture as possible of his last hours in this world, if we are to have much chance of finding out who killed him.'

'Yes. I don't think I can tell you very much, that's all.'

Methinks the young man doth protest too much, thought Bert Hook. Open University literature studies had made him prone to such quaint phrases, but he took care not to voice them among his colleagues at the station. He produced his notebook and said, 'You were one of the last people to see Mr Upson. We need to have the details of that.'

The fair-skinned, revealing young face looked immediately shifty. 'It was on a Friday. Not last Friday, the one before that.'

'So we understand. But we need your confirmation. I understand that you were seeing Mr Upson in connection with some deficiencies in your work.'

'Yes. I – er, well, I'd let myself get behind, like.'

Bert Hook, who had got up at five thirty for many months so as not to 'get behind' with his part-time studies with the OU, said innocently, 'Pressure of student life got to you, did it?'

'Something like that.' Lawson didn't seem to detect any irony. 'I – well, I didn't organise my work as well as I might have, according to Mr Upson. It's one of the skills of academic life, you know.'

Lambert said drily, 'I'm sure it is. But one you didn't have. Was Mr Upson helping you in your struggle to acquire it?'

The young man looked thoroughly puzzled. 'He was sympathetic, Mr Upson. He was trying to help me.'

'And was his confidence justified? Did you produce the piece of work he had been waiting for when you had this last meeting with him?'

'Well, no, I didn't, actually! But I didn't know then that it was going to be the last time we met, did I?'

'I see. What is your position with regard to your studies now, then?'

'Well, I don't know, really. I still haven't produced my dissertation. I've got all the material ready for it, but I missed the date, you see.'

'Which was?'

The blue eyes dropped as he looked thoroughly shame-faced. He gave them a sheepish grin as he said, 'March the thirty-first, actually.'

There was something odd about this young man, but Lambert couldn't quite work out what it was. He had continued to embarrass him about his work in the hope of pinning down what this was, but he didn't seem to be getting anywhere. He decided it was time to let Lawson off the hook and said, 'Well, we're not here to talk about you. It's Mr Upson we're interested in, as you know. Think carefully now, Jamie. Did he seem to be in any way agitated when you saw him on that Friday?'

'Friday afternoon, it was.' Lawson spoke awkwardly, almost as if he expected the simple statement to be challenged.

Hook said quietly, 'What time was this, please?'

'Three forty-five.' It seemed unusually precise, coming from this ill-organised student. Lawson watched Hook write down the words in his clear, round hand.

Lambert asked again, 'Did you notice anything odd in his bearing?'

Lawson paused for thought. 'No, I don't recall that he seemed any different from normal. The stress was on me, you know, and I wasn't noticing him particularly, except

52

that I wanted to see how severe he was going to be with me.'

'I understand that. But we are speaking of a murder victim and you were one of the last people to see him alive. Did he seem to be worried about anything? Was he giving full attention to you and your problems, or was he abstracted, with his mind on something else?'

Jamie nodded slowly, his young, mobile features suddenly full of concentration, as if he, like others before him, felt the charnel-house glamour of murder, the oldest and darkest of crimes. 'No. As far as I can remember it, Matt was pretty normal, pretty much the way I'd seen him before. But as I said, it was deadly serious for me, with my university future at stake, so I was concerned with that and my own emotions.'

Lambert sighed. 'All right. Tell us what was said about your own situation.'

Lawson looked confused, even shifty. Perhaps it was just embarrassment that his sorry tale was going to tumble out again before these impassive strangers, who could hardly be expected to be sympathetic to an errant student. 'Matt – Mr Lawson, that is – told me I'd been a fool to get myself in this situation, and a bigger fool not to heed his warnings to dig myself out of it. He couldn't allow me any more time for my dissertation and the matter would now be out of his hands. I would appear in the official lists as a failure, because the necessary work had not been submitted.'

'So that is the end of the matter? Your studies are about to be terminated?'

Jamie hesitated, then said almost apologetically, 'Not quite. There is an appeals procedure. Matt said he was now donning his other hat, as my tutor, and advising me what to do. I was to complete the dissertation over the vacation and present myself as a penitent to the appeals panel at the end of September. That was his phrase. He said he thought there was a good chance that they would say that it should be assessed, and that if it was then found satisfactory, I would probably be allowed to enter my final year studies.'

He spoke the words as though quoting from a book; he had obviously memorised the advice from his tutor. Lambert wondered how far this nuisance of a student merited all this attention, but that was not their concern. There was something eluding him about this rather pathetic paleface with the shaven head and the hunted air, but he was getting no nearer to divining what it was. He said, 'Think carefully, please, Jamie. Even though you were a student and he was a tutor, you have inhabited the same working environment for the last two years as a man who has now been murdered. I ask you this in confidence: do you know of any person or persons who might have wished him ill?'

'No.' The reply came a little too promptly, from a man who could hardly wait for the question to be completed.

Lambert let the eager monosyllable hang in the air for a moment, emphasising its haste, looking steadily into the pale blue eyes until they eventually fell. 'Do you know of any activity of Mr Upson's, inside or outside the university, which might be connected with his death?'

Lawson glanced from one to another of the watchful faces in front of him and then dropped his gaze to the floor again, all within a single second. He said stubbornly, as if repeating a formula, 'No. I was just a student and he was just my personal tutor. I didn't see a lot of Mr Upson.'

They left him standing alone on the wide, shallow steps of the high brick building, an isolated, anxious figure. It was a scene both of them were to recall many times in the weeks which followed.

The action at the coroner's court was brief and to the point. The retired police sergeant who acted as coroner's officer had thought there might be some chance of an open verdict, since there must be a possibility of suicide with a man shot through the temple at point-blank range. Matthew John Upson would not have been the first man to seek out a lonely part of the

Malverns to end the agony of a life which seemed to have nothing but pain in store.

But no weapon had been found by the body. And though it was possible that someone had removed the weapon without reporting the discovery of the body, Cyril Burgess's report about the angle of the shot was taken as conclusive evidence that this man had not died by his own hand.

The coroner, a bluff man with a military moustache and much experience of death, directed the jury firmly towards a verdict of murder, by person or persons unknown. The whole proceedings, including identification evidence by Liz Upson and the pathologist's report, took no longer than twenty-five minutes.

The coroner offered his sympathy to the grieving widow, followed by an assurance that he was confident that the police would be both vigorous and successful in their pursuit of whoever had done this.

The body was not released for burial.

One woman felt it had been a mistake to attend the inquest. This was not the place for a mistress, whether current or discarded. She could only draw attention to herself, when she could not afford to do that.

Clare Booth had told herself she owed it to Matt to be present at this last secular rite of passage, to hear how these strangers thought of the man she had loved.

But as she sat at the back of the court, listening to the dispassionate tones of the official witnesses who had not known Matt and the quiet, controlled evidence of the wife who had known him all too well, she realised that it was curiosity rather than compassion that had drawn her here. She wanted to hear the grave processes of the law in operation, wanted above all to find out how much the police had found out about Matt, about his death, and about who might have killed him.

She was disappointed. The law proceeded briskly but coolly, in an attempt to spare the feelings of those closest to the bereaved. Clare had never met the austere, dignified old lady in black, who sat still as marble, attentive as a bright-eyed bird, throughout the proceedings, but she knew at a glance that this figure of genuine grief must be Matt's mother. Clare felt she was the only person in that high, quiet room apart from herself who really mourned this passing.

As for the police, they gave nothing away, beyond the brief information in reply to a question from the coroner that an early arrest was not in prospect. And she didn't know the ways of the police: perhaps even that was a smokescreen, to put a leading suspect off his guard.

Or her guard. The bulky man in the grey suit who had sat silent and observant throughout the proceedings in the coroner's court followed her down the steps outside and spoke quietly to her before she could go to her car. 'Ms Clare Booth? I'm Detective Sergeant Hook. My superintendent is in charge of the investigation into Matthew Upson's death. He'd like to put a few questions to you. As soon as possible, please.'

There were others who were interested in the findings of the coroner's court, but they were not foolish enough to draw attention to themselves by attending, nor even by sending a minion to report back.

There were not going to be any surprises in the verdict. It was always unlikely that the coroner would accept that Upson had died by his own hand when there was no weapon present. The verdict of murder by person or persons unknown didn't bring any cold thrill to the man who read of the verdict in the *Gloucester Citizen* behind closed doors on that Thursday night. This man had seen many deaths in his time, a number of them violent; in the vast majority of these cases, no arrest had been made.

Gangland killings are notoriously the most difficult for the police to solve, and both they and the criminal fraternity know it. Contrary to popular opinion, the police are not content to ignore such deaths, happy to see villains eliminate villains and leave the world with a little less trouble in it. Police chiefs resent the view that criminal bosses should be a law unto themselves, beyond the reach of those whose job it is to make sure that the law of the land is the one that obtains for all. The police know that if they acknowledge that anyone, however powerful, can take the law into his own hands and get away with it, anarchy is not far away.

This man read the few paragraphs in the evening paper, allowed himself a grim smile, then summoned two of the lieutenants of his dark army. 'They'll have searched his house. Upson swore there was nothing there to connect him with us, and he must have been right, or we'd have heard from them by now. You went through his room in the university?'

'Yes. Last week, when he was just a missing person. Lance did it. No one saw him.'

The thickset man behind the big desk smiled. He had known it would be so. He had given his orders to that effect. But even people like him needed reassurance. Or needed to double-check, he told himself: you didn't build an empire like his without being thorough, and attention to detail was part of being thorough. He nodded. 'What about the people he had working for him?'

'They know the score. The ones we can still use are being assigned to other couriers. One or two we won't be able to use. It's going to be quiet anyway, until October.'

He nodded. The killing had been at a good time, in that respect. Other than a few locals, the students would have to get their supplies from elsewhere, over the summer. And at the end of September, there would be a new crop of youngsters, a thousand and more new possibilities for his lucrative and well-organised trade. A growth industry, despite the pious pronouncements of governments and their repeated and feeble attempts at control.

But you didn't succeed without vigilance. 'Did you check that Minter is available?'

'Yes. I used the contact number. His coded message said Minter was ready for hire. He'd like three days' notice and all the detail you can give him.' Even this man spoke Minter's name with a little awe. Contract killers might be merely the tools of the barons of this evil trade, but they commanded high prices, and money always compels respect in the world of crime.

'Right. Keep your ears and your eyes open. If the police get too close to any of his contacts, we'll need to eliminate them.'

It was always best to speak of 'we' rather than 'I' when it came to the letting of blood. It implicated others, encouraged the rule of silence.

Seven

Not many people nowadays can afford to live in houses constructed from the Cotswold stone which was once the dominant building material of Gloucestershire and Herefordshire. Surprisingly, Clare Booth, a humble lecturer in what had now become the University of Gloucestershire, was one of them.

It was in fact a modest enough residence, not far from the centre of Oldford. A nineteenth-century primary school had been replaced with a proud new modern building, large enough to accommodate the growing numbers of children in the prosperous small town. An enterprising developer had bought the original school and converted it into four small houses, each with two parking spaces in what had once been the playground. Clare lived with her handsome Burmese cat Henry in the end one of what the agent had inevitably called 'Character residences with all the advantages of thoroughly modern interiors'.

On the evening of Thursday 24 June, she sat looking out of the attractive stone-mullioned window, awaiting the arrival of the CID and trying not to feel nervous about it. She told herself that she would be honest wherever she felt she could be. That was surely the best policy. 'Don't get too friendly, Henry,' she warned the cat as the two large shadows fell across the glass of the front door. 'They're not friends, these chaps, they're here on business.'

She found it unnerving that they got down to that business with hardly a sentence of small talk. It was a perfect summer evening, and the crimson blaze of the sunset was framed by the tall stone window of her sitting room, almost as if it had been designed for that very purpose, but these two men commented neither on this natural beauty nor upon the dark gleam of her antique furniture, which usually brought admiring comments from those setting foot for the first time into her house.

Yet they did not seem unfriendly, these two. It was the powerfully built sergeant who had spoken to her after the inquest, and his leaner and even taller superintendent. They were both older than her and gave an impression of being far more in touch with the world and its evils. Well, that was natural enough, she supposed: their job must bring them into touch with the worst side of humanity. Henry ignored her injunction and jumped up on to the sofa beside Detective Sergeant Hook; within two minutes he was stretching luxuriously on the ample police lap, nuzzling his ears against the notebook above his head and purring loudly.

What Clare did find intimidating was the way the CID men studied her, without embarrassment or apology, and the way their questions seemed to be invested with overtones she could not pin down. It was as if they were working to an agenda of which she was not aware and never would be. It made her more afraid of making mistakes, less confident even in the areas where she had thought she had nothing to fear.

Lambert for his part perceived an attractive woman who was tall and had moved well as she set them in the places she had obviously arranged for this meeting. She had very black and lustrous hair, which hung in a ponytail, and a pale, oval face, whose attraction was hardly diminished by the anxiety she plainly felt. He had a theory that men with fair-haired wives chose brunettes when they chose a mistress: here was another statistic to support his thesis.

He began quietly enough. 'We need to find out all we can about a murder victim, if we are eventually to discover who killed him. Murder is the only crime where the victim can never be questioned, can never give his account of what happened. It's obvious enough, but people don't always appreciate that we have to ask very personal questions when we are trying to fill in the picture of the life a victim led.'

Clare said with nervous aggression, 'You mean you have to decide who your suspects are.'

He smiled, and she could see when the grey, intelligent eyes lit up with humour that he must have been an attractive man, when he was younger. 'No. That approach would lead to corners being cut and wrong decisions. What we try to do is to build up the most complete picture possible of the dead man and his associates, with particular reference to the last weeks, the last days, and when possible the last hours of his life. As we do so, we are able to eliminate most people we talk to from suspicion of murder. By speaking frankly, you are much more likely to rule yourself out as a possible killer than to implicate yourself. Assuming, of course, that you are in fact innocent.'

His smile broadened, removing the sting from his last statement, but his eyes never left her: her reaction to this as to everything else would be studied and analysed, she was sure. She laughed. 'Innocent until proved guilty, is that it?'

'Not quite. That's a legal term, and we aren't lawyers. Sergeant Hook and I are allowed to speculate about guilt and innocence, and sometimes we do so, with our colleagues, as the days pass and we exchange the information we acquire. But we do that in private, and the law prevents us from making any arrest without being able to justify ourselves.'

'And are you near to an arrest in this case?' She tried to be as cool as he was, but she knew that he held all the cards.

'You wouldn't expect me to answer that, Ms Booth.'

'No, I suppose not. Incidentally, it's Miss, as far as I'm concerned; I hate the sound of that clumsy Ms. But I don't think I can help you much.'

'You can help to fill out our picture of a man who was brutally murdered, or we wouldn't be here. Tell us all you can about your relationship with Matthew Upson, please. This won't go any further, unless it proves to be evidence in an eventual prosecution.'

His tone was light and friendly through all of this, so that she had to remind herself how serious the matter in question was. She coiled one of her long legs beneath her on the chair before she spoke, trying to remain calm, forcing herself to take her time. 'I first met Matt four years ago, when I came to the college. But for the first year, we were no more than working colleagues.'

'And then?'

'We began an affair.'

'A serious relationship?'

She smiled. 'Oh, it was serious, all right. As much time as we could grab together. Interminable discussions of when he was going to leave his wife.' How tawdry a great passion seemed, when you reduced it to the basic facts, she thought. But everyone thought his or her own passions were larger than other people's. 'Neither of us intended it to be that serious at the start, I think. Perhaps neither of us wanted it to, but it built up over the months.'

'And was it still going on at the time of Mr Upson's death?'

For a moment, she was tempted to say it was. It would have been the simplest line, and she found herself going through her colleagues, wondering which of them would be able to say with certainty that it was not so. But something about those cool grey eyes told her it would not be wise to deceive this man more than she had to. 'No. It was over.'

'And how long had it been over when he was killed?'

'Three months.' The promptness and the precision were a mistake, she realised, after her earlier hesitation. She watched the stubby fingers of DS Hook penning the information as Henry nuzzled insistently at his hands, threatening to dig the claws of his front paws into the sergeant's sturdy thighs if he did not get his due share of attention.

'And who ended it?'

For an instant, she was back in her teens, wanting to deny the humiliation of being ditched by some acned boyfriend. Then she sighed. 'Matt did. He said he couldn't risk losing his kids.'

'But you didn't think that was the real reason.'

He must have caught the bitterness she had striven to

keep out of her voice, she thought. It was like being with a psychiatrist. Except that this man was not here to help you. There was no guarantee here that your answers wouldn't land you in trouble. 'No. His kids were an excuse. He wanted rid of me, in the end.'

What a world of suffering, of anguished nights and agonised emotions, lay behind that terse sentence, thought Lambert. Yet he was grateful to this tall woman with the striking black hair and the eyes that were almost as dark as that hair for being so terse. The last thing he needed was a welter of tearful recriminations. He said, 'I realise that this is painful, but while I think it may have any bearing on a murder case I have to pursue it. Can you tell me more specifically why Matthew Upson ended the relationship?'

She couldn't stand the unrelenting scrutiny of those grey eyes. She stared fixedly at Henry, stretching himself luxuriantly on Bert Hook's knee and purring steadily. 'Matt had other fish to fry. Other things going on in college. Before you ask me, I don't know what they were. But he was preoccupied, this last year, even when we were together.'

Lambert wanted to press her harder on this. But she had already said she didn't know any details, and her wide mouth had set into a determined line with that assertion. She was still a person voluntarily helping the police with their enquiries, not a person under arrest, who could be questioned intensively. He said, 'And did these other interests help to break up your relationship?'

She looked as if she wished it had been so. Instead, she said bitterly, 'No. He had other women. Younger women. I was an episode in his life, not a permanent fixture, as I had imagined.'

'Can you give me names?'

She shrugged her shoulders, as if she could dismiss with the gesture the foolishness of her time with Upson. 'I'm not able to give you names. Perhaps there wasn't anyone specific.'

Lambert studied the set, blank face, knew the pain that was behind it. He said quietly, 'Students?'

She nodded, suddenly near to tears with the humiliation of it all. 'Yes. I'm sure there were students.' She glanced up into the impassive, attentive face, then down again at the cat. 'They're adults at eighteen nowadays, you know. Capable of making their own emotional decisions. It may be professionally irresponsible for tutors to exploit a relationship, but there's nothing illegal about it.'

The words had the ring of a quotation. Whose words were these originally, he wondered. Matthew Upson's, perhaps? They were uttered with the bitter irony of resentment, so that was quite possible. Lambert said gently, 'Nevertheless, I need the names of anyone you know who had any close dealings with Mr Upson in the last weeks of his life. You must—'

'So that you can drag some stupid girl who was daft enough to drop her knickers into a murder hunt? I don't think so, Superintendent!' All the weary, pointless rage of an affair gone wrong was suddenly turned upon him and his questions. She heard herself rising towards hysteria. 'I don't know names. I wasn't interested in who was the latest little tart to attract his attention!'

Henry stopped purring. His head lifted Hook's notebook and his wide blue cat's eyes focused upon his excited mistress in fearful enquiry. Lambert listened to her breathing as she tried to recover control. 'When did you last see Matthew Upson alive, Miss Booth?'

'On the Wednesday before he disappeared. We were in a meeting together. About changes to next year's courses. We didn't speak afterwards.' The words tumbled out in quick succession, as though they were ones she had prepared and rehearsed and were anxious to get right. But then, even an innocent person might well have anticipated this as a standard question – especially if she was intelligent and interested as this woman.

Lambert's eyes had never left her face. His final question came as calmly as all his other words as he said, 'Did you kill Matthew Upson, Miss Booth?'

She strove to recover control. And knew as soon as she

spoke that she had failed. 'No. No, I didn't. And I don't know who did. But I hope whoever pulled that trigger gets away with it!'

Two women close to Matthew John Upson. Two women who were happy to admit that they were glad he was dead. Lambert reflected as they drove away that he could not recall such a thing before.

It was Bert Hook who said, 'I felt she was holding something back. She knew more about his activities in that university that she was telling us.'

When they reached the Murder Room at Oldford CID, they found proof that these mysterious other activities of Matthew Upson's might have been lucrative ones.

DI Rushton, coordinating the activities of the twenty-three officers now engaged in the investigation, had turned up an interesting piece of evidence about the dead man. The initial search into his financial affairs had revealed nothing unusual. His salary was paid into a branch of NatWest within three miles of his home, and the joint account with Elizabeth Upson had the usual direct debits and standing orders to ease the conduct of their domestic affairs. The figures were totally unremarkable, with nothing in them to suggest a marriage that was heading for the rocks.

Now Rushton had turned up something else. It was an account in the name of John Matthew Upson at the Halifax plc office in Ross-on-Wye. The reversal of forenames was a common ploy in people seeking to conceal the existence of such accounts, and the fact that Ross-on-Wye was twenty miles from both Upson's residence and his place of work reinforced the view that he had wanted to keep the existence of this particular account secret.

So did the details of the account itself. It did not reflect the economic life of a university lecturer. It had begun with a deposit of five thousand pounds, twenty-nine months before Upson's sudden death. By the time of that death, the credit balance in the account was just over two hundred thousand pounds.

Eight

Liz Upson claimed she knew nothing of her late husband's bank account in Ross-on-Wye.

They met that strange mixture of well-bred surprise and earthy contempt for her dead husband which they had noted in her before. 'Of course I didn't know about Matt's private nest egg. That was the point of him hiding it away in Ross, wasn't it?'

That was logical enough. Lambert, studying her closely, still felt that this was not completely a surprise to her. 'You didn't have any hint from his conduct that he was salting away considerable sums of money?'

'I told you, he was an arsehole!' She glanced at Bert Hook's round, experienced yet strangely innocent face and said with a coquettish smile, 'At least, I told Detective Sergeant Hook here, didn't I? I think he was quite shocked by the fundamental nature of my language at the time. But I expect your investigation is proving me right, isn't it?'

Lambert said stiffly, 'Your views on the character of your husband are not relevant to this issue, Mrs Upson. His salary was going into your joint NatWest account. Have you any idea how he might have been acquiring large sums of money from other sources?'

'No. Matt was an Arsehole with a capital A, and I had long since ceased to take any interest in his activities.'

'So you've no idea where this money was coming from?'

'I'm happy to say I haven't a clue. He came and went as he pleased. So long as there was enough money to pay the bills and look after the children, I didn't give a damn about him.'

'I see. Well, in view of your feelings about him, it may not upset you to hear this: unless there was some legacy of which none of us is aware, it seems doubtful whether your husband could have acquired such sums by legal means.'

Liz Upson brushed her fair hair away from her left eye, a gesture that was more one of exultation than alarm. 'So he might have been not just an arsehole, but a crooked arsehole. Wait till old Mother Tindrawers hears about that. I'd love to be a fly on the wall when you tell Mrs Hoity-Toity Upson about the activities of her beloved son.' A note of craft stole suddenly into the light-skinned, attractive face. 'You said large sums of money. How large?'

Lambert thought quickly. This flinty woman was still the next of kin. It was her legal right to know about her husband's assets, whatever their relationship had been at the time of his death. 'There was over two hundred thousand pounds in the Halifax account. I believe there is half-yearly interest due to be added to that.'

Liz Upson's face lit up, seemingly with amusement rather than greed. 'Which, in the absence of other claimants, would come to his wife, I suppose?'

'I can't pronounce on that. You would need to take legal advice. And if there was any crime involved in the acquiring of this money, it might well have to be returned to the parties who have been wronged.' But even as he spoke, he did not think this sum had come from theft or fraud.

She smiled. 'So there is a strong possibility that the late and grieving wife of Matt Upson might come in for a nice little windfall. Sorry, a nice big windfall! There is every chance that that useless arsehole will be worth far more to me and the kids dead than he ever was alive.'

The laugh which followed this was still ringing in their ears as they drove disconsolately away.

The solution to the enigma of Matthew Upson's mysterious riches must surely be found at the place where he had worked.

The new part of the campus of the University of Gloucestershire seemed a pleasant place as Hook drove the car up the long drive. The Georgian stately home which was the administrative centre of the complex stood four-square and handsome at the end of the half-mile ribbon of tarmac between the avenue of two-hundred-year-old limes. The newish halls of residence, none of them more than four storeys high, blended surprisingly well into the parkland landscape, helped by the majestic chestnuts and oaks which had been left wherever possible among them.

A cynic might have said that the site's gracious attractions were enhanced by the scarcity of students. On this sunny day of high white clouds and bright blue sky, the majority of those who had not already finished their studies for the year and departed to summer employment were either in the examination halls or studying feverishly for the morrow's trials. Even the Head of Matthew Upson's Department, Elwyn George Davies, seemed less harassed without the hum of student activity about him. 'Another year almost over, another year nearer to pension!' he said as he sat down with Lambert and Hook in his office. They suspected it summarised his attitude more than his jesting tone allowed.

Lambert decided to shake this complacency. 'We've unearthed a large sum of money in a secret account of Mr Upson's,' he said briskly. 'It seems almost certain that it came from some illegal activity. An activity which was probably based here, at his place of work. We'd like your views on what that source might have been, Dr Davies.'

Contrary to the view of popular novelists, very few people who are taken aback actually splutter. George Davies, Ph.D. and Dean of the Faculty of Humanities, did. A series of inarticulate noises were accompanied by irregular discharges of saliva. For Bert Hook, it was a moment of relief in a trying day. As a man who had spent his boyhood in a Barnardo's home, he still liked to see figures of authority discomfited. Davies eventually dabbed at his chin with an off-white handkerchief and produced, 'You cannot be serious!'

John McEnroe, 1984, thought Lambert. Perhaps this man, like the tennis player, should have been checked at an earlier stage of his career. Aloud, he said, 'I'm afraid I'm perfectly serious. I'm not suggesting that you yourself have been involved in any criminal activity, Dr Davies, but I've a shrewd suspicion that your late colleague Matthew Upson was.'

Davies clutched at the straw of his personal innocence; it seemed to restore to him the power of rational speech. 'I certainly am not aware of any such thing. I shall be surprised if any of my staff have been involved. But I suppose it is your duty to explore all avenues, however grubby they may be. You will appreciate that my role in the Faculty is confined to academic administration. I am not as close to my staff as I should like to be, owing to the burdens now placed upon me, and I have certainly no jurisdiction in anything beyond academic matters.'

Lambert would like to have had some fun with the old windbag, but he decided that duty must prevail over light relief. 'I understand that. Perhaps you could put me in touch with someone who knew Mr Upson as a teaching colleague. Someone who saw him on a day-to-day basis, and who might be more aware of his activities outside the lecture and tutorial rooms?'

Davies looked at him suspiciously through narrowed eyes. He said abruptly, 'Charles Taggart.'

Lambert, who had left the choice open to see if Davies would come up with another name, was a little disappointed. He noticed he hadn't suggested Clare Booth; perhaps Davies wasn't even aware of the relationship which had lasted for two years and more between two members of his staff. He said, 'Is Mr Taggart in the university today? There don't seem to be many people around.'

Davies diverted them to his secretary in the outer office, and they got some brisk and efficient action immediately. In under two minutes, she had tried Taggart's personal tutorial room, the Senior Common Room, and his home, and located him at the last.

Lambert offered to drive out to see him, but Taggart said he would meet them in forty minutes in his tutorial room, leaving them wondering why he did not wish them to come to his home. Policemen are professionally curious, sometimes professionally cynical. There were a number of possible reasons why he should wish to meet them here, most of them perfectly innocent.

Lambert refused the secretary's offer of tea, much to Hook's unspoken disgust. The two of them wandered blinking into the bright sun outside. The few students who were lying individually or in pairs with books looked up at them curiously from the grass. Perhaps they thought they were parents, come with the family car to take away the bulky necessities of student existence, like television sets, hi-fis, computers, even the occasional couple of books. More likely the worldly wise youth of the new century recognised them as plain-clothes coppers, thought Hook: they didn't look friendly.

Then he realized that this wasn't a desultory stroll to pass the time. They were at the hall of residence where they had met James Lawson, the defaulting student who had been one of the last people to see Upson alive. They passed through the deserted entrance hall and up three flights of stairs at an accelerating pace. Bert tried to disguise his panting, in the face of Lambert's scarcely affected breathing. He didn't know that his chief had felt a familiar stab of pain in his chest outside, that he was attempting to shrug it away from mind as well as body with this physical exertion.

They found Lawson's room without difficulty: he had told them he lived on the top floor, and the names were on the doors in neat brass slots. Lambert rapped sharply and they heard a muffled noise from within, the sound of something falling. Lambert threw open the door and walked in.

James Lawson lay face downwards on the bed. His head had turned towards the door at the sound of the knock, the book which had been lying face down beside him had slid on to the floor with that movement. He looked amazed by this sudden presence in his room, like a man aroused from a deep sleep in the middle of the night. But this was four o'clock on a bright June afternoon.

'I said we might need to speak to you again, Jamie,' said Lambert breezily, 'and here we are.'

The young man peered at them blearily, too confused even to register hostility. He swung his legs cautiously to the floor, held his forehead between his hands for a long moment. 'I told you all I could tell you when I saw you last time,' he said dully, without moving his hands.

'I don't think so, Jamie. Things have moved on since then.' Lambert motioned to Hook, who walked over to the window and opened it to its widest, letting some air into the stifling room.

Lawson shivered, crossed his forearms across his chest, stared resentfully not at Hook but at the window and the curtain moving softly in the breeze. 'I was having a kip,' he said unnecessarily.

'As a rest from your intensive labour in getting your dissertation completed, I suppose,' said Lambert, glancing at the blank pad of paper on the table to his left. He pulled out the upright chair from beneath the table and sat down heavily, leaving the room's single armchair to Hook and his notebook. Lawson stared dully at that object as Bert turned ostentatiously to a new page.

As he tried to collect his senses, the boy became more defensive. 'Had a bit too much to drink at lunchtime,' he said with an attempted smile. 'One of my friends was off for the vac and we had a couple of pints. Then I must have dropped off.'

Lambert studied the white face while the words dried up. The boy took a gulp of air, tried to frame another thought. But before he could speak, Lambert said harshly, 'You weren't drunk, Jamie Lawson. You were drugged. I could do you for possession right now, if I wanted to. Maybe more.'

Lawson was in no shape to conceal anything. His eyes darted automatically to the chest of drawers behind Hook, and they knew in that moment that they had him. His gaze

71

flicked from one to the other of the two big men who had arrived so abruptly into his room. 'It was only a bit of pot,' he said defensively. 'We all do it. All students do it. You must know that.'

'Not all, Jamie. Not even a majority. And you do more than pot, don't you?'

Again the swift, desperate shifts of his eyes, like a cornered animal seeking escape from a predator, told them more than words. He said desperately, 'You said yesterday you were interested in Matt Upson. Why aren't you chasing a murderer, instead of persecuting a small-time user like me?'

'Oh, but we are, Jamie. The trouble is, you see, that we're beginning to find out things about the late Mr Upson. Things which may involve you.'

'I don't know what you mean. I can't help you. I'm admitting to using a bit of pot, but nothing more.' His face set like a child's in denial.

Lambert did not take his eyes from the young face as he said, 'Have a look in those drawers, will you please, DS Hook.' He saw the fear start into the widening eyes, followed by a hopeless apprehension as Hook drew open the bottom drawer.

Removing the thin disguise of underpants and socks, Bert withdrew polythene bags, with smaller bags inside them, placing them on the table beside the blank writing pad with slow, relentless care. Jamie Lawson watched his movements as though hypnotised, then looked back at Lambert, willing him to break the tension in the room, which was still warm but which felt to him so cold.

It seemed a long time before the Superintendent reached to the nearest packet, drew aside the top, sniffed it to confirm what he already knew. 'Cocaine, Jamie. Enough for a serious pusher, not a user. Enough to put you behind bars, for years. You're in real trouble now, aren't you?'

This time there was no denial. Lawson had ceased even to look at his tormentors. His eyes were on the floor. Presently there came a sound which tugged at the heart of Bert Hook, whose own boys were at the opposite end of adolescence from this broken boy-man. It was the low whine of weeping.

Whatever flimsy resistance there had been was broken now. Lambert said gently, 'You were supplying this to students on the campus, weren't you?'

A nod, an attempt to speak which never reached the mouth, a hopeless sagging of the shoulders. 'And who was supplying you, Jamie?'

A vigorous shaking of the bent head, as if he could jerk away this nightmare. Lambert's calm voice, as relentless as the flow of a stream, pressed on. 'It was Mr Upson who fed you what you needed, wasn't it? You were his pusher here, weren't you?'

Silence for a moment, then a despondent nod, still without the head being raised. 'One of them.'

'And where did he get the coke from?'

'I don't know. Honestly, I—'

'And why was he killed?'

'I don't know. I was as shocked as anyone when he disappeared. I didn't think he was – well, I . . .' His words petered out and he lapsed again into tears.

Lambert glanced at his watch. They were already late for their meeting with Charlie Taggart. He looked back at the abject, incoherent figure in front of him. 'Have you any more of this stuff around?'

The weeping figure shook its head; the hands remained clasped over the face.

Lambert said, 'We shall take this away and weigh it, Jamie. We shall be back in the morning. There will be charges, very serious charges. What happens to you is out of my hands, but it will be affected by how much help you are able and willing to give to the people who question you. I advise you to consider your position very carefully indeed.'

They saw the top of the head nodding its assent. Lambert was reluctant to leave him like this, but the combination of drugs and emotion meant that that he would produce nothing more than wild and whirling words about the shadowy drug world behind these bags of innocent-looking white powder. Meantime, the murder of Matthew Upson, which might or might not be related to this scene, awaited investigation.

Jamie Lawson looked up as they were at the door. He held out a thin, supplicating hand for a moment, then dropped it. Lambert said impatiently, 'What is it, Jamie?'

'It's just that I – I – oh, nothing!' He threw his face into his hands in disgust.

Lambert looked at him impatiently for a moment, then at Bert Hook, who had found a Sainsbury's bag to give anonymity to his odd burden. 'We have to go. We'll see you tomorrow morning, Jamie. Early.'

They could hear the soft keening from behind his door even when they reached the end of the corridor.

Nine

C harlie Taggart's tutorial room was a comfortable place. One wall was lined from floor to ceiling with well-filled bookcases. Foliage plants and a number of small glass ornaments in brilliant blues and greens gave individuality to a room which might have seemed anonymous. There was a large desk and a filing cabinet, but a window which extended almost from floor to ceiling let in plenty of light to glint on the glass. It also afforded a pleasant view over the fields at the edge of the site. Sixty yards away, a Hereford cow chewed meditatively and stared over the fence at this latest manifestation of man.

Much to Bert Hook's delight, there was a pot of tea and a plate of biscuits waiting for them. 'It wasn't difficult to arrange,' said Taggart when they thanked him, 'there aren't too many people around today to call upon the refectory's services.' If this was a reference to being called back into work at four o'clock on a Friday, he gave no signs of being annoyed.

He seemed, indeed, more alert and friendly than when they had seen him three days earlier, when he had on his own admission been suffering from a hangover. His still pale face was considerably more animated, his startlingly black and undisciplined eyebrows moved unpredictably as he handed them their tea and biscuits. 'I gather from the phone call that things have moved on in the Matt Upson investigation,' he said.

Since it was obviously possible that a friend of Upson's might well have been involved in the dead man's illegal

75

activities on the campus, Lambert had been watching for signs of anxiety since they had entered this comfortable room. So far there had been none. He tried to surprise Charlie Taggart. 'We've just been talking to Jamie Lawson.'

The lecturer was pouring the last cup of tea for himself. The stream of amber fluid did not waver. He said, 'And did you get much sense out of Matt's recalcitrant student? I hardly know the lad myself.'

A careful disclaimer. Yet although he had never taught the boy, he had known immediately whom they meant. Lambert asked him why.

Taggart wasn't ruffled. 'I'm afraid the Lawson man has been a notorious backslider throughout this year. You get to know the names of students like that, even if you don't have to deal with them yourself. Their names tend to come up at Faculty meetings. You get a kind of advanced notice that you might have to consider their academic futures at the end of the year.' He smiled. 'I found a missive intended for Jamie Lawson put in my pigeonhole by mistake earlier in the year – an official warning that my course might be terminated if I didn't pull up my socks, as a matter of fact. I had to check the envelope before I realised it wasn't meant for me. That kind of thing tends to pin up the name on your mental noticeboard.'

Irrationally, Lambert found himself irritated by this man's urbanity. Taggart knew this academic world far better than he did, and was making the most of it. 'And did any errant missives arrive from the people who were using Jamie Lawson to peddle cocaine around the campus?'

This time he had surprised him. The black eyebrows flew high and the deep-set eyes looked up quickly as the steaming tea was forgotten. 'Pushing drugs, was he? The young fool! Well, it's no surprise to find students using drugs these days, I'm afraid, but I'm appalled that anyone should be pushing the hard ones among his companions. Students know the risk of hard drugs, better than most.'

'And it comes as a surprise to you that Lawson should be involved in this way?'

'A complete surprise, Superintendent. I told you, I hardly know the lad.'

Lambert wondered how much that 'hardly' covered. 'Would you be equally surprised to hear that Matthew Upson was involved in the distribution of drugs on this site?'

Taggart paused for thought, looking from one to another of the expectant faces. Then he sighed. 'No, I wouldn't, Mr Lambert, to be perfectly honest with you. I would never have called myself a close friend of Matt's. But in the last eighteen months or so, we've become less close.'

'Did you have some kind of disagreement?'

He smiled and shook his head, his plentiful dark hair moving vigorously. 'No. Nothing like that. I just saw less of him, that's all. We'd occasionally had a drink together, swapped information about was going on, enjoyed a bit of mutual whingeing over the blindnesses of our masters. You know the kind of thing. Well, Matt seemed to become preoccupied with other things. Clare Booth, for one. We just didn't seem to find the time to get together, lately. I regret that now: I suppose you always do, when someone dies suddenly.'

Lambert wondered if he was deliberately distancing himself from a man he had just been told had been involved in illegal activities. But they had found nothing as yet to connect this man with the drugs operation; Jamie Lawson certainly hadn't mentioned him, but they might find more out from the student on the morrow, when his brain might be fully alive to his dire situation. 'Were you aware of a serious problem among the student population?'

Taggart shrugged his shoulders beneath his dark green short-sleeved shirt. 'What is "serious" nowadays? I knew there was a certain amount of drug-taking, of course. Some of the students talk about highs now as we used to talk about drinking sprees in my student days. And I understand it's now cheaper to get high on cannabis than on alcohol, which seems dangerous, to me. But where I've come across it, I've assumed there was nothing more serious than pot involved.'

'And that really is as much as you know about it?'

The dark, deep-set eyes stared him evenly in the face. 'It is. I come in here each day, do my job to the best of my ability, and go home. If you want to know what goes on round here at nights, you should talk to the resident wardens of the student halls of residence.'

It was a fair enough point, but it sounded, as he delivered it, like a prepared statement. Lambert said, 'We shall be doing that. And I've no doubt young Mr Lawson will be able to give us lots of information as well, in the morning, when he realises the seriousness of his situation.'

For the first time, he got a reaction, fleeting but definite. Some emotion – whether excitement, or fear, or merely interest, it was impossible to say – flitted briefly across the heavy features of the pale face. Then Taggart said with an effort, 'I shall be interested to find out what has been going on, and no doubt I shall, in due course. Particularly as you say Matt Upson was involved.' He paused, then said thoughtfully, 'Jamie Lawson was one of the last people to see Matt alive, wasn't he?'

'Yes. On that last Friday afternoon. Just after you, apparently.'

If he saw anything insulting in the reminder, he chose not to react to it. 'Just after Matt refused to go for a drink with me, yes. I think I told you that when we last met. You haven't found anyone who saw Matt after that?'

'No one has admitted seeing him, no. It may be of course that whoever he was meeting killed him. We're now pretty certain he was dead by the end of that Friday.'

'It could have been these drugs people, couldn't it?'

'That's a very vague phrase, isn't it? But understandably so. The people who make the big money out of what is a dreadful but highly lucrative trade keep themselves very anonymous. And you're right: it's a highly dangerous trade to become involved in. People who are in a position to help the Drugs Squad often die mysteriously. That's why it's essential that you tell us anything you can think of that connects Matt Upson with the supply of illegal drugs.'

Charlie Taggart gave the matter serious thought. 'I'm sorry, I can't help you. What you say makes sense, as soon as I hear it. Matt did seem to be busy with other things. He didn't seem to be as concerned about his job and its problems as he'd been when I first knew him. I thought he was preoccupied with things in his private life. But he did seem suddenly much more affluent.'

'Did you see him at any time with people from outside the university? People who might have been involved in the supply of drugs?'

'No. I'd like to be able to help you, but I can't. I told you, I saw less of him in the last year or two, and what I did see was on the campus, mostly with students and other members of staff.'

'If anything occurs to you in the days to come, please contact Oldford CID immediately. It may be that now that your mind has been set running on this, things or people may seem significant which passed you by until now. But please keep this information to yourself: we don't want people put on their guard. Remember that drug dealers are not only involved in an evil trade but may include the person who ended the life of your friend Matt Upson.'

Taggart nodded, agreed to think hard, listened to their warnings about playing amateur detective. When they had gone, he sat for ten minutes in his chair without a movement. Then he made a single phone call. 'They think Matt died on that Friday night. And they know he was involved with the supply of drugs.'

His voice was carefully neutral. It would have been impossible to decide from his tone whether he thought this was a good or a bad development.

Friday night, and nearly eight o'clock. The sun was sinking on a balmy summer evening, gilding the ridge of the Malverns

79

in the distance. All breezes had dropped away, even on the highest part of the golf course at Ross-on-Wye. A wonderful, calm English evening, as peaceful and as soothing to the spirit as anything in the world.

'Bastard bloody game!' said Bert Hook, 'Bastard, bastard, bloody STUPID game!' He beat the turf with his 5-iron and considered dispatching it after his golf ball into the undergrowth. Then he trudged on morosely, feeling the blood pounding in his head, a balanced, equable man, reduced by the trials of this slow, quiet game to a murderous lunatic.

John Lambert affected not to hear him. He had had a stab or two of that chest pain again, on the first hole, but it had gone now. He must concentrate on helping Bert, who was quite new to the boons of this wonderful game. 'Great way to unwind after a trying week, this,' he said reflectively, 'just a quiet two-ball as a superb evening moves towards dusk.' He played a smooth 8-iron and smiled appreciatively as it bounced at the front of the sixth green and rolled gently towards the flag.

He'll be telling me about rhythm next, thought Bert darkly.

'You don't seem to have your rhythm right tonight, Bert,' said Lambert. 'I should concentrate on that, if I were you.'

Hook looked round. There was no one in sight, for it had been after seven o'clock when Lambert had enticed him out for what he had called 'a quiet nine holes'. He could kill the man quietly – perhaps beat him to death with his favourite 7-iron, the only club he knew he would not miss with – and be away. But experience told him that the circumstantial evidence would point strongly to him. And if he was tried by a non-golfing judge, even his plea of the mitigating circumstances of Lambert's insufferable air of superiority on the course might not be given its proper weight. He contented himself with a glare of molten hatred at the back of his companion and trudged miserably after him.

Lambert expostulated on the virtues of the softly hit 8-iron he had just produced before asking with an air of bafflement what had happened to Hook's ball. 'Out of bounds!' growled

Bert through clenched teeth. 'Again! Bastard, bloody stupid FUCKING game!'

Uniquely among policemen, Bert Hook had never been heard to use the f-word at work. Now he was reduced to it by a game we are regularly assured is a wonderful source of relaxation and a means of reducing tension in men of his age. Lambert shook his head sadly. 'You're still hitting at the ball instead of swinging,' he said sagely. 'Keep trying, and it will come, all of a sudden.'

'Like diarrhoea. And just about as useful.' Bert stared sourly at Lambert's ball, refusing to be cheered even when a short putt ran round the rim of the hole and stayed out.

But the goddess of golf changes her affiliations as readily as the most promiscuous trollop. Bert was able to play his favourite 7-iron at the short seventh, and his unbelieving eyes saw the ball roll to within a foot of the hole for a certain two. Lambert could not keep the astonishment out of his 'Good shot!' but Bert walked to the green with a new tread, the modest gait of a man who did these things all the time and expected no less.

On the long eighth, John Lambert slashed his ball wildly right into the trees. 'That was a shank!' he said, staring down unbelievingly at his club.

'Yes. It's been threatening for some time,' said Bert loftily. 'You've been getting too close to the ball. Try watching the ball extra closely. But try to stay relaxed.' He had to turn his head away from his opponent on the last phrase, so that the smile he could not control would not be visible.

He won the hole, of course. And then he won the ninth, when Lambert fluffed a chip from just off the green, allowing the novice Hook to shake his head sadly and offer a little more advice. 'You decelerated the club as you came into the ball. It's a very common fault. Everyone does it, at times.'

Lambert stared at him suspiciously, since it was the advice he had offered to Bert the previous week, returned to him word for word. But Bert had his back to him, returning his putter carefully to his bag after winning the hole. Incredibly,

Lambert had lost the last three holes and they were all square after the nine holes he had proposed. 'The light's holding and it's quiet. We'll play on to thirteen,' he said grimly.

Bert didn't argue. He moved swiftly to the tenth and dispatched a long, straight drive between the tunnel of trees to the distant fairway. 'Sorry I didn't speak, John. I was anxious not to lose my rhythm,' he said.

When Lambert pulled his drive savagely into the trees on the left, he thought he would maintain his dignity by refusing to sink to the lurid language of his sergeant. He moved down the fairway in silent fulmination. It was left to Hook to comment. The normally taciturn figure found it difficult to hold his peace on the golf course. 'Stupid bloody, game, isn't it?' he consoled Lambert. 'As I said earlier.'

The sun was now well set. Lambert insisted on him holing a two-footer for the extended match in the gloom of the thirteenth green. Bert bought him a pint and discoursed to the steward on the excellence of his game and the fallibilities of his superintendent's. He had forgotten all about the cares of the working week, he said: that was one of the advantages of this game. It could be trying at times, but you had to stay with it, keep your patience, wait for things to happen. Talent would out eventually, if you gave it free rein.

Lambert offered a selection of monosyllables and moved rapidly to a second pint. That pain in his chest had been there again when they started. And then it had disappeared, just as Bert was becoming unbearable.

When he got home and sat in a darkening room with the television flickering like a magic lantern in the corner, he was quiet for a long time. Then he said to Christine, 'Your suggestion that I should introduce Bert Hook to golf. I'm not sure it was such a good idea.'

Ten

The ground was becoming parched. There had been no measurable rain now for sixteen days, and in these longest days of the year the sun was beginning to dry flowerbeds and brown closely mown grass.

But it had been a still night, and the heavy dew of the early morning disguised the dryness that lay beneath it. When John Lambert walked in his garden at seven o'clock, most plants seemed still full of the lush growth of spring. It was surprising how often he found himself out here at this time in the morning when he had a puzzling case. On winter mornings, when the clouds hung low and it was scarcely light, he could hardly understand why he came to the furthest reach of the plot, except that he was conscious of a superstitious drive to take the forces of evil as far away as possible from his family, even when he was doing no more than thinking about them.

This morning, he felt only a straightforward relief after a troubled night. He had woken up at three o' clock with the pain in his chest again, and slept but fitfully after that. It was a Saturday, and all the world seemed asleep save him. He could hear the lambs which were now almost sheep calling invisibly through the still air from fields which must have been a mile away.

But there was a blessed absence of even a distant hum of motor traffic, that sound which is a perpetual accompaniment to modern life for so many. He picked up a few tiny apples which had fallen from his trees with the June drop, then removed the first side-shoots from the dahlias, which had sprung up so fast in the last ten days. Then he dallied pleasantly, removing the odd dead flower and passing as slowly as he could among the roses, whose scent was sharp and clean in this earliest and best part of a summer day.

Christine was in a housecoat in the kitchen when he dawdled his way back into the bungalow. 'You should be resting,' he admonished, in what had become a ritual since her heart bypass operation six months earlier.

'"A normal life", the medics said,' she reminded him, 'and normal has always involved ministering to your every need, hasn't it?'

'It's a Saturday. You should be having a lie-in. And anyway, there's not much in the way of ministering to be done, since you cut out bacon and egg and proper milk for the cereals.' The old grumble, which both of them had long since ceased to take seriously. He doubted if he could manage the bacon and egg and fried bread he had consumed with such relish as a young DC, even if it was presented to him now. He wondered if others conducted the prolonged minuet of marriage with similar backings and advancings, whose Pinteresque undertones were undetected by any save the participants.

His musings were interrupted by a phone call from the station sergeant at Oldford. 'That student you went to see yesterday afternoon at the University of Gloucestershire, sir. Wasn't his name Lawson?'

'Jamie Lawson, yes.' After his deliberate slowness of the last hour, Lambert was suddenly impatient.

'He's dead, sir. Just been found. Hanged himself in his room, apparently.'

Detective Inspector Chris Rushton sometimes thought the hours like this were the best of all. It was still not nine o'clock on a Saturday morning and he was alone in the Murder Room. There was ample time to digest all the information being brought in from the twenty-eight uniformed and CID officers now involved in the Upson investigation, then to assign it and cross-reference it on his computer files. The chief wouldn't be in for a while yet, if at all; Superintendent Lambert was certain to go out to the university campus, where that student bloke who had been pushing drugs had now topped himself. Rushton made himself a big mug of coffee and sat down contentedly before his computer.

It was while checking the house-to-house reports and the statistics from the beat cars active in the area of the Malvern Hills on the day of Upson's death that he came up with something interesting. It showed the benefits of his cross-referencing system, because it was only when he set the information from car sightings beside that from the enquiries made on the site at the University of Gloucestershire that something interesting popped up.

He had no great hopes from the car sightings. The period involved was not precise enough to offer anything significant. Officers had been asked to inform CID about any non-local cars seen between ten in the morning and midnight on 11 June around the minor road which ran along the western base of the Malverns. This was where Upson's body had lain, but because the corpse had not been discovered until ten days later, it had not been possible at the outset of the investigation to be more precise about the time of death.

It now seemed likely that Upson had not died until the late afternoon or evening, so Rushton was giving particular attention to the later sightings. The car which caught his attention was one of several which had been seen more than once in the area during the day. Most of these had been eliminated as belonging to people who were going about their normal Friday business. This one had caught a young PC's attention because of a prominent sticker indicating support for the Dewsbury rugby league team, an unlikely slogan to glimpse in the Malverns.

The registration number showed that the car, a three-year-old black Vauxhall Vectra, had begun life in Yorkshire. Nothing very odd in that: cars changed ownership and moved around the country. But the check with the DVLA at Swansea showed that this car had changed hands only once, and that change had been in the same town where it had originally been registered. The second and presumably present owner was a Harold Rees of Ossett, near Dewsbury, in Yorkshire.

It was at this point that Rushton's cross-referencing came triumphantly into its own. The information about the black Vectra was part of a mass of detail which in the old days might have overwhelmed a murder case team, causing them to miss a tiny but significant connection. But when Chris now fed in another mass of apparently unrelated information, that gathered by the officers who had been assembling the details of all Upson's students at the University of Gloucestershire, he cross-referenced it, and found a surprising link.

This was a first-year history student named Kerry Rees, whose home was in Ossett, near Wakefield, in Yorkshire. Her course work had been eminently satisfactory for most of the year, though it was too early for any results of the first-year examinations she had just completed. Kerry Rees had finished her programme for the year and gone back to Yorkshire.

But arrangements had already been completed at the time of Upson's death for Kerry to suspend her course for a year. The reason was that she was currently pregnant and did not feel she could continue to study effectively through the months of the pregnancy and those after the birth. She had refused any suggestion of a termination.

There was no record of who the father might be.

Around the entrance to the hall of residence, a ragged line of students stood in near silence, whispering occasionally to each other, keeping a respectful distance from the glass double doors, watching the comings and goings of the vehicles and the people who had an official connection with this death.

In the little cube of a room on the top floor which had been Jamie Lawson's home for the last year, the Scene of Crime team had almost finished its work when a grim-faced John Lambert arrived. They had cut down the body, which lay face down on the floor, mercifully obscuring the rigid and tortured face which Lambert remembered in vivid young life on the previous afternoon.

Sergeant Jack Johnson, veteran of many an operation such as this and Lambert's long-time colleague at Oldford, took in his anguish at a glance. 'You couldn't have known it would come to this, John.'

'I should have foreseen it when I spoke to him yesterday. He was upset then. I left him to stew in his own juice until his brain cleared. Thought it would bring him to his senses.' He smiled mirthlessly at the bitter irony of that, as he stared down at the senseless form on the floor of the room. In the top branches of the ancient oak outside, unexpectedly close to them, a rook cawed harshly, as if in mockery of this tangled world of man.

Lambert said dully, 'One of the parents will have to do an identification. Have they been informed?' He was going through a ritual, searching for a routine to follow in the attempt to allay his own pain.

Johnson nodded. 'Parent. There's only one. His mother. The marriage broke up years ago, apparently.'

They were silent for a moment, thinking of the pain to be brought into the life of this anonymous woman, who probably knew nothing of her son's lifestyle here and the death it had brought him to. Lambert wondered how he could have missed the signs, how the normally sensitive Bert Hook could have failed to notice the depth of the distress that had led to this. And they had gone off to play golf, at the very time, perhaps, when . . . He wanted to shout that aloud, to relieve the pain of his guilt by making it public. He understood in that moment the relief which Catholics might find in the confessional.

The civilian photographer signified that he had taken all the pictures he needed and departed quietly. Johnson walked over to supervise the man dusting the single window sill with white fingerprint powder, more to break the tension with Lambert than because his attention was needed. Lambert stared unseeing at the familiar activities going on around him, his mind back with the interview in this room on the previous day, wondering what he might have done to prevent this tragic consequence.

If he hadn't been in such a hurry because he was late for his meeting with Charlie Taggart he might have noticed the depths of the boy's distress, might have appreciated the wretchedness and desperation which was closing in upon him.

He forced himself back to the present. 'When did he do it, Jack? Early this morning?' He was torturing himself now, picturing the boy's misery building through a sleepless night, until there seemed no way to end his misery save the desperate method he had adopted.

Johnson shook his head without turning round. 'He died last night, John. He was stone cold when we got here at eight.'

Had he not been so preoccupied with his own distress, Lambert would have known from the clipped monosyllables that the grizzled Johnson was concealing something, waiting for it to be drawn forth by questions, as if to volunteer it would be in some way indecorous.

'The police surgeon's been?' For the first time he could remember in his career, Lambert was speaking for the sake of it, trying desperately to get his own emotions back under control so that he could proceed rationally. He knew perfectly well that the police surgeon would already have been here. However obvious death might be, however cold this young corpse might have been when found, death had to be confirmed with an official signature. That was the first part of the very routine he was striving to re-establish for himself.

Johnson turned at last. 'Yes. He's in the room next door, as a matter of fact. I think he was planning to write a note for you.'

Lambert looked at him for a moment, then glanced sourly at the fingerprint powder on chairs, desk, drawers and wardrobe. 'Fat lot of good that will be. But I suppose you have to go through the motions.'

Johnson's face was troubled. He did not smile back. Instead, he said insistently, 'I think you should have a word with the police surgeon, next door.'

Lambert took a last look at the shape which had yesterday been Jamie Lawson and turned abruptly away.

The doctor was a young man, not more than thirty. He was sitting at the student desk and contemplating his report. Lambert was surprised how hoarse his own voice sounded as he said, 'I'm told he did this last night. Not long after I left him, then.'

The doctor didn't have a lot of experience, but he recognised the sound of someone who wanted to punish himself. He said formally, 'Death certainly occurred some time before midnight, yes. Perhaps the post-mortem will give you something more precise.'

Lambert shrugged. 'It hardly matters with a suicide. The point is that I should have realised—'

'There's one thing you should know right away, Superintendent. This wasn't a suicide.'

Lambert heard himself repeating the words stupidly, as he had heard many a shocked relative do in the past. 'Not a suicide?' Then came a sort of relief as his brain resumed its normal mode, his mind clicked into operation like a machine that had been jammed. 'You're sure of that?'

'Absolutely sure. That boy next door was dead when whoever did this strung him up.'

Eleven

The Drugs Squad has more autonomy than any other section of the police service. It needs it, for it is fighting the biggest criminal empires in the modern world, as challenging to the law and far more widespread than the American gangster networks of the twenties and thirties. When it is fighting such forces, the law needs a flexible and swift-moving army, able to use the appropriate tactics for a particular situation.

The problem for the police struggling to control an industry which is better financed and more tightly organised than their own multifarious service is to get at the generals of this vile army. The newest copper on the beat can arrest users of drugs, and it is relatively easy to pick up the first tier of suppliers: people like Jamie Lawson, often users who are drawn by their need for coke and heroin into becoming retailers of drugs to other users. But usually the tongues of such operators are tied by fear of reprisals, and even if they are willing to talk, often they do not know the people who are providing their supplies, just as this next tier of men and women do not know – and sometimes take care not to find out – the next rank above them. It is a criminal industry which thrives upon anonymity.

Even a superintendent in charge of a murder enquiry must sometimes defer to the advice of the Drugs Squad, for he must not imperil the brave men and women who take it upon themselves to infiltrate the networks which import and distribute the range of drugs which are the currency of this evil but lucrative trade. But murder is still murder. It is the worst crime, given the highest priority, and the British police are proud that it should be so.

It was Sunday morning when John Lambert rang the man in charge of the Drugs Squad in the West Midlands, but the voice with the vestigial Birmingham accent on the other end of the line was instantly alert. He knew he wouldn't have been bothered at home on a Sunday unless something important was afoot. His first instinct was to protect his own team, but he knew as he listened to Lambert's calm, succinct account of his problem that he must give whatever assistance he could.

This man had an overview of an area which stretched south-west from Birmingham to Bristol. It was not a complete picture, or he would have been able to move his army in and win the war. He saw himself as fitting in more and more pieces of a highly complex jigsaw. If and when the picture became complete, or even almost complete, it would be time to move in.

The problem was that this puzzle didn't obey the first rule of jigsaws: the picture you were assembling didn't stay the same as you worked upon it. But two people involved in the supply of drugs had been murdered: he knew as soon as Lambert spoke that he must give him whatever information he had about the drug situation in the area where this killing had taken place.

'It's part of Sugden's empire. But only a small part, on the fringe. It's no use your going to see Keith Sugden. He'll deny all knowledge, and there's no way we can even show he's connected, at the moment.'

Lambert sighed. He knew the man well, and would have loved to have pinned a murder on him.* 'Who, then?'

A pause. Releasing information came hard, even in this situation. 'Kennedy. Do you know him?'

'No.'

'He's a small guy, trying to get big. Sugden's using him

* See *An Unsuitable Death*, by J.M. Gregson (Severn House, 2000).

to run his operation in Gloucestershire. He might move him up, if he's good enough.'

Just like an ordinary firm, a straightforward commercial enterprise, thought Lambert. A young executive who might go on to greater things if he did his present job diligently and listened to the chairman's dictates. 'Where's he based and what's his cover?'

The two questions you always asked about anyone operating successfully in the drugs world. Again the voice on the other end of the line hesitated a fraction before it said, 'Simon Kennedy's based on your patch. And he uses three dry-cleaning shops in Cheltenham and Gloucester as his cover.'

'I'll have to see him. Will I put anyone in danger when I confront him about this death on the university campus?'

A longer pause. Then, 'No. He's well aware that we know about him, but the difficulty is proving his connection with drug distribution. He doesn't store anything on his shop premises and we haven't traced his chain of supply yet. We haven't a scrap of evidence that we could take to court. But the important thing for you is that we haven't any of our people planted close to him. You're not likely to blow anyone's cover by grilling him. In fact, if you could pin this killing on him, it could only help our work – we might be able to scare one or two of his associates into talking.'

Lambert smiled grimly into the mouthpiece. 'Thanks. I'll do my best.'

But this man Kennedy had so far been more than a match for the considerable resources and intelligence of the Drugs Squad. Even if he had ordered the killing of Jamie Lawson, it wasn't going to be easy for anyone to prove it and bring him to justice.

Rushton gave his news of the new addition to the leading suspects in the Upson murder at their conference on Sunday afternoon. Lambert and Hook had come into the station to allow the Inspector to bring them up to date on the latest intelligence from the team and to offer him what they could on what was now established as the murder of Jamie Lawson.

Rushton's enthusiasm for his own suspect, the zeal for a possibility which was very much his own finding, was a little dampened by Lawson's death. 'Harold Rees was probably driving his own car on that Friday: his daughter was in an exam during the afternoon and his wife doesn't drive. But the snag with him as a suspect is this second killing. Assuming the two murders are connected, we'd have to prove that this man Harold Rees came down here again to kill Lawson,' he said glumly.

Lambert smiled. 'You did well to turn him up, Chris. He'll have to account for his presence down here on the day of Upson's death. And we'll need to see his pregnant daughter and find out who the father of her child might be. It's possible the deaths of Upson and Lawson aren't connected. If they are, it's the drugs business which seems the strongest link.'

Rushton nodded. 'We've got the full report from Forensics on the bullet which killed Matthew Upson. They're the right calibre and the right degree of distortion to have been fired by Upson's own pistol, which is missing from his house. A Beretta. Without having the weapon itself, of course, no one can be certain, and we all know it's highly unlikely it will ever be seen again.'

Hook said slowly, 'So it looks as if he took it out that day because he thought he might have to defend himself against someone, but in the end had it turned upon him.'

Lambert nodded. 'That's the likeliest scenario, but there are other possibilities. For instance, he might have given the pistol to Clare Booth at some time, for some reason unknown. Only to find her transformed from lover to discarded mistress, with vengeance in mind.'

Rushton, who had not seen any of the people interviewed, said, 'We only have Mrs Upson's word for it that she was surprised to find the pistol missing. She could have used it herself.'

Lambert nodded. The forceful Liz Upson had made no

secret of her dislike for her husband. He had thought at the time that she would hardly have spoken so frankly had she been involved in his death, but her scatological contempt for the man she had insisted was an 'arsehole' might have been designed for that very purpose. Her hatred of Upson would have come out anyway – the dead man's mother would have made sure of that – and the frankness she had insisted upon might have been no more than an acknowledgement of that.

Rushton was checking his files again. 'Upson was seen by both Charles Taggart and Jamie Lawson on the afternoon of Friday the eleventh of June. Those are the last recorded sightings. If we accept the view of the forensic entomologist that he died later that same day, his wife is in the clear. She was with her children from when she picked them up from school, and there are witnesses to that.'

'So we would have to assume that she paid someone to kill him. It hardly seems likely. She's a tough woman, but hardly one you'd expect to have access to contract killers.' Lambert shook his head slowly. 'How comprehensive is this list of car sightings, Chris?'

'Nothing like comprehensive, I'm afraid. It's almost entirely random. The patrol cars in the area only recorded people they thought interesting for one reason or another – mainly vehicles which were not local and were seen more than once during the day. Hence Harold Rees's Vectra. The house-to-house people have asked local residents for the vehicles seen around the area where the corpse was found, but of course this was after the discovery of the body, at least eleven days after the day in question. I'm afraid the list of sightings is very unreliable, with huge gaps inevitable.'

Lambert nodded sadly. 'We still have no idea of how Upson got to the Malverns on that fateful evening. He didn't drive his own car there: that was in the garage for service.'

'And he didn't take a taxi, as far as we've been able to check. None of the local firms reports a fare to the Malverns answering Upson's description on that day. And they'd be likely to remember, because it's not a usual destination for them.'

'So the likeliest thing is that he didn't meet his murderer there, but was taken there by him – or her. Willingly or unwillingly.'

Hook said, 'If he was carrying his own gun, he must have been afraid of someone.'

Lambert pursed his lips. 'Or threatening someone. Don't forget he'd a lot to keep secret. He was dealing drugs in a big way. He was a sitting target for a blackmailer, for instance. It's possible that he was threatening someone else with the pistol when it was turned upon him.'

Rushton said gloomily, 'The team seems to have gathered a huge amount of information without it taking us any nearer to our killer.' He rolled back the cuffs of his immaculate white shirt. He was always smartly dressed, even though he had lived alone since his divorce three years earlier. In a situation where many policemen became unkempt, less careful of their appearance, Rushton was if anything more spruce than ever.

He hated untidiness, and this was an increasingly untidy case.

There was a new Porsche in the drive of the big, rather brash mock-Tudor house. The manicured lawns and regimented flowerbeds spoke of a professional gardener. The small maroon blazers on the chair in the wide hall behind the man who opened the door to them were those of the most exclusive private school in the area.

A man of Kennedy's age and background couldn't have made money like this except from crime, thought Hook. From drugs, to be precise.

Lambert had shown his warrant card and introduced them brusquely on the doorstep, then strode without apology into the deserted room to the right of the front door where Simon Kennedy had indicated reluctantly that they might talk.

'Shouldn't you say you're sorry to have to disturb me at

home on a Sunday night?' Kennedy motioned to the two armchairs at one side of the room and made to sit with his back to the window.

Lambert was too quick for him. He moved into the chair the man had been planning for himself and motioned to Hook to sit beside him. Kennedy hesitated, then sat down opposite them. A shaft of evening sun shone suddenly as a high white cloud moved on, gilding his young face, seeming to emphasise how he had missed out on the opening move in this bizarre game. 'We can do this at the station, if you think it preferable,' said Lambert.

Kennedy leaned a little to one side, so that the sun would be less in his eyes. He would have got up and drawn the curtain, but he was obscurely aware that it would have been a defensive gesture. He was twenty-eight years old, trying to hold himself upright and look taller than he was and more secure than he felt. He had an earring in one of his small, delicate ears. The effect of his well-cut dark hair was rather destroyed by the ridiculous triangle of jet-black beard he affected on the point of his chin; this curious patch of hair was so flat that it looked as though it had been painted there with tar.

Kennedy said, 'We'll do it here, now that you've come. Whatever it is, it can't take long.'

'A student at the University of Gloucestershire, James Lawson, was murdered on Friday night.'

Kennedy raised his thin eyebrows, too high, like a bad actor. He looked like a man trying to play a villain in Jacobean drama, thought Hook, fresh from his Open University studies: *The Duchess of Malfi*, perhaps. Except that this man was too young and too inexperienced to play such a villain convincingly. Kennedy now said, 'Really? The local paper said he was found hanged. I rather assumed the young fool had topped himself. One less parasite to support from our taxes, I think I said to the wife at the time.'

Lambert's face tightened a little round the mouth. 'James Lawson was supplying drugs to the students on campus. He

96

was too high on coke to speak to us reliably, on Friday. But he was going to tell us all about it on Saturday morning, when he had been warned to be in a fit condition to talk to us. But someone prevented that happening.'

Somewhere at the back of this big modern house, an infant cried, a strange, plaintive, innocent sound to provide the backcloth to their discussion. Simon Kennedy said, 'Well, I'm sure this insight into how the other half lives is very interesting, but I fail to see—'

'You were supplying him, Kennedy. He was going to tell us all about you, if he'd been allowed to.'

It was a hit, a palpable hit. They could see in his eyes that the thrust had found its mark. And Lambert knew in that moment that this man would never cut it with the big boys of his evil industry. Keith Sugden would have smiled them away, would have shown how foolish was their accusation by the very absence of any swift reaction. This man tried bluster. 'Look, you'd better be able to show some reason for an accusation like that. If I chose to—'

'You deny it?'

'Of course I do. I'm a respectable businessman. Three shops of my own and growing. If you think you can—'

'Works well as a cover, does it, the dry-cleaning business? Can you show enough turnover to launder all the thousands you're making from coke and heroin? I doubt it, if we called for a detailed audit.'

'You'd better be careful just what you're saying. This is harassment of an honest businessman! You must know that.'

'So bring an action! Complain to the Chief Constable! Take me to court! Put your drugs money where your mouth is.' Lambert was chancing his arm, knowing he could not prove the connection of this man with the murder of Lawson, perhaps not even his connection with the drugs: if this was part of Sugden's empire, the traces would be well hidden. But he had had a long and trying day and lost most of his weekend, and his patience with it. His contempt was real enough, and it was stronger than the will behind the young face opposite to him.

Kennedy spoke a little too loudly, with the conviction dying in his voice. 'I'm a successful entrepreneur. You plodders wouldn't understand that! I know the dry-cleaning business, and I'm building up an empire in it.' He folded his arms across his thin chest; his expensive leisure shirt seemed suddenly too big for him.

'You're saying all this came from three small shops?' Lambert's glance of disbelief took in the house, the Harrods curtaining, the carpet, the furniture.

'I don't have to account to you for where my money comes from. I'm an entrepreneur.' He repeated the grand word with a flourish, as if they had not taken enough account of it the first time, but it fell flat for the lack of a reaction.

'You may have to do just that, in due course. Account for where all this comes from. In the meantime, you can tell me about how much coke, heroin and cannabis you supplied to Jamie Lawson and others.'

Having failed with bluster, Simon Kennedy tried the would-be-reasonable note. 'Look, Superintendent Lambert, I realise you have a very difficult job – and you too, Sergeant. This drugs culture is a terrible thing, and there must be some awful people involved who are making fortunes out of it. But I assure you you've got the wrong end of the stick here. I don't know who gave it to you and I don't expect you to reveal your sources, but if I find who it is, I shall take the appropriate legal action. I can only think it may be some smaller and less successful business rival – you'd be surprised how cut-throat things can be sometimes.'

It was a long speech, and it carried less conviction as he went on. He had expected to be interrupted, and the fact that these two men heard him out phlegmatically gradually unnerved him, until he ended with a nervous giggle. Lambert regarded him steadily for a few seconds after he had finished. Then he said, 'Why did you have Jamie Lawson killed?'

Kennedy was visibly shaken, as the big boys of this trade

where killing was common would not have been. Keith Sugden, the man at the summit of this empire, would have been impassive, unflustered, oozing rather than displaying contempt for the police machine which could not touch him. Simon Kennedy was none of these things. He jutted the absurd scrap of beard defiantly at them as his face paled. 'I didn't have anything to do with this death. You won't be able to fix it on me.'

Hook looked up from his notebook, tightening the screw which Lambert had begun to turn. 'We won't need to fix anything on you, Mr Kennedy. It's obvious this boy was killed because of his drugs connection. Someone wanted to shut his mouth for good before he gave the game away. That someone could only be the man who was providing his supplies, couldn't it? Look at it from our point of view for a minute, and you'll see how things stand.'

There was something near panic now in Kennedy's wide brown eyes. He had taken Hook for a solid plodder, a time-server keeping his nose clean and waiting for his pension, not someone who would come in with such relish with the threat of arrest. He felt his own voice waver as he said, 'I didn't do it. I didn't kill that wretched student myself and I didn't pay anyone to do it for me.'

Hook smiled at him. 'Difficult to believe, that is. Be a pity for you if it happened to be the truth. This is murder, you see. Mandatory life sentence. Then there'll no doubt be supplementary charges, relating to the supply of drugs.' He shook his large, ruddy face sadly. 'Going to be locked away for an awful long time, Simon. Of course, if you could say the orders came from above, that you were in complete ignorance of what was going on, you might just get away with it – providing you could give us the evidence to charge one of the big boys, of course.'

'I've told you, I don't know anything about this. The first thing I knew was when I heard it on Severn Radio yesterday.'

Lambert pursed his lips, allowing the silence to press in

further on the clearly alarmed Kennedy. Again there was a small child's cry from the rear of the building. 'Be a pity if you didn't see anything of those children until they were adults – and even then, they wouldn't want to know you when you came out.' He decided they had got as far as they were going to get by bluff, which was all he had really been able to use. He was sure that this man had been supplying drugs to Lawson, as the Drugs Squad superintendent had told him, but even of that, they had no tangible proof as yet. He stood up. 'Get yourself a lawyer, Mr Kennedy, and fast. You're in deep trouble. One of your own, not one of Keith Sugden's. You need someone who will tell you what's the best course of action for you. And he'll tell you what you already know: your best policy is to make a clean breast of things and get out as lightly as you can.'

The clearly apprehensive Kennedy stuttered a repetition of his innocence. As Lambert left the room, he made a belated attempt to establish some sort of rapport with Bert Hook. 'I've seen you somewhere before, Sergeant. I think I know where now . . . Did you used to go into schools to talk to adolescents?'

Bert looked at him. 'I used to talk to youngsters about the dangers of drugs, yes. About twelve years ago. I probably spoke to you. Pity you didn't listen.' He followed Lambert to the front door. Then, as his chief stepped off the single step and moved back to the car, Hook turned back to the pale face and the too-revealing brown eyes. 'If you killed Jamie Lawson, we'll be back to arrest you. If you didn't and you survive this, get out of this game, lad. We'll get you in the end. And if we don't, the likes of Keith Sugden will. You're not hard enough for them: once he finds that out, he'll eliminate you, like a man swatting a fly. Get out while you can!'

Simon Kennedy attempted a smile of contempt at the puniness of the CID before he shut the oak front door. It was wasted, because neither of the officers looked at him again.

He went back into the empty room where he had spoken

to them and slumped into his chair. Twenty minutes earlier, the murder of Jamie Lawson had seemed like the solution to a problem. Now, it seemed to be opening the trapdoor to a dark void beneath him. He sat for a long time with his head in his hands.

Twelve

The doctor was young. She looked about eighteen to Lambert's jaded eye, but he knew she must be at least twenty-four. He had asked for the earliest possible appointment and said any doctor would do. So it was his own fault that he was stripping off his clothes at eight o'clock in a surgery which was only just warming up.

The girl did not make any conversation whilst he was behind the screen. In a moment he stood awkwardly before her, stripped to the waist, trying not to think how much younger she looked than either of his own daughters. He flinched and giggled nervously at the coldness of her stethoscope as she sounded his chest and back; her serious air, which made him wonder how often she had done this before, how many other ageing bodies she had observed in their decline.

'Breathe in and hold it, please,' she said sharply, and he took the deepest breath he could, straining like a schoolboy to expand the chest beneath these slim, asexual fingers.

She tapped his chest and his back and listened to her stethoscope, asked him questions about his diet, nodded her approval when he said he had given up smoking ten years and more ago. She took his blood pressure and muttered that it was satisfactory, almost as if that was a disappointment to her.

Then she asked for a lot of detail about the severity of the pain and the exact times when it had occurred. She asked if his job involved him in a lot of stress and whether he sat behind a desk all day: he said no to both and she nodded several times. Then she looked at him with her head on one side for a second, like a bird assessing a not very attractive worm. He was torn between admiration of her thoroughness and a nagging fear that she might already be certain that this was something serious.

John Lambert wasn't used to being ill. It was a long time since he had presented himself to any doctor, and he realised that he had unconsciously been expecting some reassuring, dark-suited man of at least his own age. When she finally allowed him to get dressed, he fell to wondering whether this pretty, serious girl was nerving herself to tell him something awful when he emerged from behind the screen. The thought meant that he had difficulty fastening the buttons of his shirt.

The doctor was writing at her desk when he emerged fully clothed and sat down on the chair opposite her. This was what people must feel like when he interviewed them, he thought, as he speculated nervously about what would come next. She had put on a pair of glasses with small round lenses to write, but they didn't make her look any older. He waited a second or two, watching the small hand scribbling furiously. Almost against his will, he said anxiously, 'I expect it's nothing serious. Bit of a waste of your time really, but my wife said I should come and have it checked out, you see!'

She put down her pen carefully, like a sixth-former finishing an exam, and gave him the first real smile she had allowed herself since he came into the room. 'Your wife was quite right, Mr Lambert. Persistent chest pain should never be ignored. You seem to be in generally good health, for a man of your age.' She made him sound like a senior citizen, he thought. He realised then that she was speaking slowly and clearly, like a woman making sure she got through to a geriatric. 'I'll make arrangements for an ECG at the hospital. You haven't had an electro-cardiac examination before, have you?'

'No. Just routine police health checks. They've always said that I was in rude health.' Again that nervous giggle was out before he could suppress it.

103

'There isn't a long delay on ECGs. They'll call you in the next few days, I should think. I've marked it as urgent.'

Urgent! He must be at serious risk, if he was being rushed through the National Health Service system like this! He'd be in intensive care by weekend. Rushed off for a bypass operation. For a heart transplant, maybe. If it wasn't already too late for that.

He became aware that this attractive, unlined angel of death had taken her glasses off, was standing smiling behind the desk which looked so much too big for her, waiting to dismiss him. 'Just routine, Mr Lambert. Nothing serious, in all probability, as you say. But it's always as well to have these things checked out.'

He walked carefully past the rows of curious eyes in the waiting room, installed himself into the driving seat of his car with elaborate care. He didn't want that pain coming on again.

Four hours later, Lambert got out of the car and levered himself painfully upright after the long drive to Yorkshire.

'You look like an arthritic heron,' said Bert Hook, watching his passenger easing his long legs cautiously back into movement.

'And when did you last see an arthritic heron?' said Lambert grumpily. 'No respect for rank, that's the trouble with the modern police force! Anyway, you hardly look like the lithe young fast bowler who used to frighten batsmen around the Minor Counties circuit.'

'That's why I'm reduced to golf,' returned Bert with feeling. 'Bloody stupid game for geriatrics, golf is!'

'People like Tiger Woods, you mean?'

They looked around them, taking in their surroundings with the automatic observation of policemen, having acquired the habit twenty years and more earlier on the beat. This was a very different world from the one they had visited on the previous evening to interview Simon Kennedy.

There were rows of solid houses in smoke-blackened stone,

and even the newer terraces and semi-detached brick houses were crammed close together. Perhaps on the outskirts of the town there were isolated examples of spacious modern residences like Kennedy's mock-Tudor detached house, but if so they were well away from the spot where they stood, which was within half a mile of the centre of the small town. Here there was still the odd mill chimney, probably no longer functional, which bespoke the older industrial heritage of wool, and the days when the workers had perforce to live close to the gates of the factories and mills which dominated their lives.

The Rees house was one of a row of these older stone houses. It was not one of the humblest, for it had a tiny front garden, which blazed with busy Lizzies. No one disturbed the neat green curtains at the windows, but someone must have noted their arrival, for the blue-painted front door with its brass knocker was opened before they could knock. A grey-haired woman in a pinafore said, 'I'm glad you're not in uniform; they talk about visits from policemen, around here. You'd best come in. Dad's waiting for you in the parlour.'

'Dad' proved to be her husband, Harold Rees, the owner of the three-year-old black Vauxhall Vectra which had been seen twice around the western base of the Malverns on the day when Matthew Upson had been killed there. He was a heavy, stocky man, dark skinned and dark haired, a retired miner who somehow looked as though he had adapted to life beneath the ground.

It was his wife who introduced him as a retired miner, and he dismissed her after the minimum of introductory pleasantries. He looked after her as she shut the door carefully and shook his head. 'Redundant, not retired,' he said shortly, as he motioned to the two easy chairs in the crowded, comfortable room. 'Shoved out, ten years ago, I was. There's no pits left round here now. Been shut ten years and more. Most of 'em didn't even put up a fight. Put money in some people's hands and they lose their brains. Those youngsters saw a few thousands in redundancy money and didn't look more than six months ahead. Some of them are still without work.'

Each successive statement was delivered like an accusation. He stumped stiffly to the sofa opposite them and sat down heavily, his left leg held out awkward and straight before him. Catching Hook's glance, drawn automatically to that limb, he said with more pride than resentment, 'Pit accident, 1981. We were living over at Barnsley, then. They gave me a job on the surface and a couple of thousand compensation. I'd have been better being libelled than crippled, wouldn't I? Leastways, I would if I'd been Jeffrey bloody Archer!'

Somehow, they got the impression that Harold Rees might not be a Conservative voter. Lambert said, 'You have a daughter, Kerry Rees? Student at the University of Gloucestershire?'

'Ay, what if I have?'

'You were in that area, I believe, on Friday the eleventh of June.'

A pause, then, 'Aye. That was the day.'

'Will you tell us why you were there, please?'

'That's my business. Private business.'

'Not any more it isn't, Mr Rees. We're here in connection with a murder investigation. There can't be any private business, when it becomes involved in our enquiries.'

Rees glared at them from beneath his heavy black eyebrows: despite the fact that he must have been over sixty, he reminded Lambert with his aggressive jutting of the head and his bristling demeanour of drawings of nineteenth-century barefist pugilists, the men for whom the Queensberry Rules had eventually been invented. But he did not reject their argument. Instead, he said, 'It's that bugger Upson, isn't it? The one who's been murdered. I read about it. Well, serves the bugger right, as far as I'm concerned! I'd like to have killed him myself.'

'But you're saying you didn't?'

'I've said nowt yet, have I? But seeing as how you seem

to be asking, no, I didn't. Might have, though, if I'd got hold of the bugger on that Friday.'

'Perhaps you can see, then, why we have to ask you to account for yourself. Matthew Upson died on that Friday. And your car was seen in the area.'

The broad forehead furrowed in a deep frown. 'Nay, you can't have me for that. He died a lot later'n that Friday. A week at least – perhaps more'n a week.'

'No, Mr Rees. His body was not discovered until ten days after his death. But we now know that he died on the day you were seen in the area. He died, in fact, very near the spot where your car was seen on two occasions.'

Rees stared at them for a moment as the implications of this for him sank in. Then he said inconsequentially, 'I know that area quite well. My father was Welsh, you see. Moved from the Rhondda to the Yorkshire coalfield when I was a lad, didn't he? Thought the prospects were better up here.' He smiled sourly at the bitter irony of that thought now.

'Why were you in the Malverns on that day, Mr Rees?'

'Stopped there in the morning to think, didn't I? I'd driven nigh on two hundred miles. And I went into Malvern for a bit of lunch. Not that I wanted much, with what I had on my mind. But I remembered the town from years ago, see? I knew it when I was a lad, and I took Rosemary for a holiday there, years ago. Before our Kerry was born, that was.' For a second or two, his dark eyes glistened with the happiness of a time long gone.

Bert Hook looked up from his notes and said quietly, 'We know about Kerry, Mr Rees – about her condition, I mean.'

It was the right phrase to use with Harold Rees, thought Lambert. Other, more aggressive coppers would have used some phrase like 'in the club' and inflamed this old-fashioned man with their coarseness about his only daughter. But Bert's carefully chosen and rather antiquated phrase hit the right note for Rees. He looked at Hook's comfortable, concerned face and nodded. 'It was him I was down there to see. I expect you know that, too.'

Lambert smiled. 'No, Mr Rees, we didn't. But that's what we're here to find out about. Tell us, please.'

'There's not much to tell. I had an appointment to see him at one o'clock, in the Red Lion at Ledbury.'

'Who made this arrangement?'

'He did. He said it would be better if we met somewhere away from the university site. Too bloody right it would!' Rees had the air of a man who had been baulked of his prey by the man's untimely death. But as with that other and very different suspect, Liz Upson, they had to take into account that his open contempt for the man might now seem the best front for a murderer. This solid, physical man, who seemed to exude a potential for violence, could hardly have simulated any liking for the man he had so patently loathed.

Lambert said, 'Matthew Upson was the father of your daughter's child, wasn't he, Mr Rees?'

'Aye. And I wanted to know what he were going to do about it, didn't I? You don't put a girl up the duff and walk away from it.' He spat the coarse phrase that he would have objected to on other lips as part of his contempt for the man who had wronged his daughter.

'And what did he have to say for himself?'

'Bugger all. He never turned up.'

'So what did you do then?'

Harold Rees looked hard into Lambert's lined, observant face, wondering how much those grey eyes already knew of his movements on that day. Then he said impatiently, 'I waited until two. When he hadn't shown up then, I went to the university, didn't I? Well, he'd had time enough to find me, if he'd wanted to. Found where his room was, when I'd asked around a bit. He wasn't there either.'

'So what then?'

'I asked a few people, but no one seemed to know where he might be. The students were all on examinations, and there weren't many lecturers about. I'd have gone to his home address, but I didn't have that. I think I drove around a bit, then went back to Ledbury and the Red Lion, to see if they'd seen anything of him. They hadn't.'

'You didn't try to see your daughter?'

He shook his heavy head. 'No. Kerry was on exams that afternoon. That's why I'd chosen that day to meet her bloody tutor. She didn't know anything about it, at the time.' There was a sudden urge to protect his daughter, as if she might be contaminated by any suspicion that fell on him.

'But she knows now?'

He nodded. His involuntary glance at the ceiling told them that the girl was upstairs in the house.

Lambert regarded him steadily for a moment. 'Mr Rees, it seems that Matthew Upson was on the university site that afternoon, but rather later than when you were looking for him. One of his students saw him at around three forty-five on that day, and a fellow tutor saw him briefly just before that.'

'Pity I didn't wait, then. I never saw the bugger.'

'Mr Rees, did you in fact see him and take him out from there to the place where he was killed?'

'No. Course I didn't.'

'Did you meet him eventually in the Red Lion at Ledbury – or anywhere else for that matter – and take him to the isolated spot on the Malverns where he died?'

'No. I've told you I didn't. I don't even know where he died.'

'But you've already said you know the area well.'

'Not that well. And what would I have killed him with? I don't have a gun.'

'You remember how he was killed, then?'

'The newspapers said. And the television. And I was interested. I'm not going to forget how that bugger died, am I?'

'Obviously not. As you have said, you had good enough reason to wish him dead. Did you pull the trigger on that pistol, Mr Rees?'

'No. I told you. I don't have any pistol.' Rees stared

defiantly into those grey eyes, which seemed to him to be looking into his very soul.

'It seems that Matthew Upson was killed by his own pistol, Mr Rees. Possibly drawn in self-protection and then turned upon him by some assailant.'

Harold Rees was not without imagination. He saw the scene put before him all too vividly. The two men struggling violently among the waist-high bracken of the Malvern slopes, the grunting of effort on both sides, the sudden violence of the shot, and the silence which crept back into the rural scene as one man lay dead upon the ground. For the first time since they had sat down, he found it difficult to breath. The old trouble was with him, the coal-dust rattling in his lungs, as he said, 'I didn't do it. I might have done, if I'd got my hands on him and he'd tried to laugh off what he'd done with Kerry. But I didn't.'

They could check his story with the pub at Ledbury, and perhaps find someone who had seen him in the early afternoon at the university site. If they found anyone who had actually seen him with Upson on that day, it might be damning. Lambert looked at him for a moment, waiting to see if he would add anything. It was often when people tried to gild a lie, to make it more convincing in some way, that they gave themselves away. Harold Rees, breathing heavily with that rasping sound, added nothing more.

Lambert said quietly, 'We shall need to speak to your daughter, Mr Rees.'

'I don't want Kerry brought into this. She has enough problems already.'

'She is in this already, Mr Rees. She is pregnant by a man who has been brutally murdered. We have to speak to her.'

For a moment he looked as if he was going to deny them. He would certainly like to have done so. Then he nodded reluctantly. Glowering his unhappiness from beneath those beetling black brows, he said, 'I'll get her. I shall want to be present with her, mind.'

He stood up and stumped away into the hall. At a nod

from Lambert, Hook followed him. The girl must have been waiting for the summons, for she was on the stairs almost before her father called her. She glanced into Harold Rees's troubled face, squeezed his forearm, and said, 'Best if you go and sit with Mum in the kitchen for a while, Dad.'

This great bear of a man obeyed his daughter as meekly as any lamb. He hesitated at the end of the dark hall and looked round at them, with his hand on the kitchen door. The girl had already slipped through the doorway of the sitting room, but Bert Hook said firmly but not unkindly, 'Better if you leave her to say her own piece, Mr Rees. They're adults at eighteen, you know.' He followed the girl into the room and shut the door firmly behind him.

Kerry Rees had her father's dark hair, above smaller features and a delicate white skin. Her face was rather too square for classic beauty, but was undoubtedly attractive; the most striking feature was her long eyelashes, which were the more noticeable for being apparently moist at this moment. Despite the loose-fitting clothes she wore on this warm day, the curves of her figure were evident. There was nothing to tell them at first glance that she was over three months pregnant. Probably as she grew into middle age she would replicate the stocky, powerful build of her father, but at present she was undoubtedly nubile, the stuff of young men's erotic dreams. And of one rather older man, Matthew Upson, it seemed.

Lambert introduced himself and Hook and began slightly diffidently. 'Can you confirm for us the details of your pregnancy, please?'

Diffidence proved to be the right tactic. She looked at him curiously for a moment and then became a woman helping a clumsy man out of his predicament. 'Certainly. I'm fifteen weeks gone now. I can be completely accurate, because there was only the one occasion when I could have conceived. And yes, I'm absolutely certain that Matt Upson was the father. There are no other possibilities, you see.' She gave them a bleak smile.

'Thank you. That makes things very clear. And presumably Mr Upson knew about this?'

The smile moved from bleak to arctic. 'Yes, he knew. He said I was a little fool for not being on the pill.'

The bitterness with which she spat the phrases came oddly from those young lips: she was obviously quoting the dead man's words. They could visualise him clearly as she said it: worldly wise, cynical, trampling roughshod over the sensibilities of this girl who was so much less experienced in these things than he was.

But had it really been as simple, as straightforward, as that? The dead are never allowed to account for themselves, to put their own case against their accusers at the bar of moral rectitude. For all they knew, this girl might have set out to lure him into bed, might then have been using her pregnancy as a tool to attempt to ensnare him in one of life's many bizarre games.

Lambert said, 'So Matthew Upson seduced you and the—'

'Not seduced. That's an old-fashioned word, isn't it? I was a willing enough partner, at the time. Perhaps I mistook a few signals. I've no doubt that's the way he would put it, if he were still around.' She glanced down automatically at her stomach and the unseen child within it, as if she thought it important for the sake of that tiny human presence that she was honest about this.

'What signals, Kerry?' asked Bert Hook, and, as often happened, his gentle, fatherly attitude succeeded where other approaches would have failed.

She looked from one to the other of the two men who had come so far to see her, weighing in her mind whether it was necessary for her to go into these details, and then decided that it was. 'I knew he was in an unhappy marriage, which according to him couldn't go on much longer. He said he hoped we had a long-term future together. No doubt you know the sort of thing.' Her bitter smile might have been at the duplicity of all men or merely at her own harshly shattered naivety.

'But his attitude changed when he found you were pregnant?'

'Yes. But no doubt he would say that he was consistent all along, that I had misunderstood his intentions.' Again that bittersweet smile. 'He said I was old enough to look after myself, that I should have taken precautions. Then he offered to pay for an abortion.'

'Which you refused.'

'We don't believe in abortions in this family, Superintendent Lambert. To us, it's murder.' She stared him steadily in the face, challenging him to take up an argument he had no intention of becoming involved in.

'You must have resented his attitude.'

'I did. For a few days, it shattered me. But then I picked up the pieces and got on with life.'

Lambert doubted whether it was as simple as that, whether even now she was quite as calm and organised as she was presenting herself. He said insistently, 'But for those few days at least, you must have burned with an intense rage against the man who seemed to be turning his back on you when you most needed him.'

She shrugged: the mirthless smile was now certainly at her own expense. 'That's a fair summary, though it seemed much more a confusion of emotions at the time. But I didn't kill Matt Upson.'

Lambert answered her smile, trying to relax her: tension could mean an instinctive denial, an automatic refusal even to think about the possibilities he now had to raise. 'No. I don't believe you killed Matthew Upson. We've checked, you see.' The shocked, white face, smooth as fine china, seemed about to protest, and he raised his hand a few inches to prevent it. 'We have to, Kerry. Murder is a serious business. We found that you were elsewhere, and with other people, at the time he died. You were in an exam during the afternoon and with your friends during the evening. However, there is another person who was around on that day, whose movements we have not been able to check on yet.'

'Dad.' The single, intimate monosyllable dropped quietly into the comfortable room.

'Yes. No one is accusing him. But he was in the area on the day of the murder, looking for a man he had every reason to hate. We need to eliminate him from our enquiries, if we can.'

She thought for a moment, looking even more apprehensive as the implications of what she had to say dawned upon her. 'I can't help you with that. I didn't even know he'd been down to the university on that day. Not until afterwards.'

'He says he had a meeting arranged with your tutor in Ledbury. One which Mr Upson did not attend.'

'If he said that's what happened, that's the way it was. He's straight, my dad, whatever else.'

He wondered what that last phrase covered. Mulish obstinacy in the face of an adolescent daughter's rejection of his curfew times? Or something more sinister in this context, like uncontrollable fury in the defence of that daughter? 'Tell me, how soon after his visit did you find that he'd been in Gloucestershire and Herefordshire on that Friday?'

'Not until I'd finished my end-of-year exams and come home. Mum let it out. She was worried about what he might have done.'

Her hand flashed to her mouth as she realised the implications of that phrase; her gaffe and reaction would have been comic, if the situation had been less serious. 'I don't mean that she was worried about him killing Matt, I mean she was worried about the rumpus he might have caused when he crashed into the university. We didn't even know that Matt had been murdered, then.'

'But you knew he was missing?'

'Yes. The news had drifted around the History Department by the time I completed my exams and left. But we didn't hear about the death for another two or three days after I came home.'

It was Bert Hook who said quietly, 'And what then,

Kerry? Did you begin to think that your father might have killed him?'

'No! I told you, Dad would never do anything like that. I'd have known if he had!'

The denial was absolute. But the image which remained in their minds as they drove through the terraces of tightly packed stone houses and out of the old town was of Kerry Rees's uncertain and fearful white face.

Thirteen

While Lambert and Hook drove down the M1, things were happening in the criminal world they strove so hard to control.

The drugs empire has a chain of command almost as complex as that of the police, but this chain has neither bureaucracy nor weak links to hinder its efficiency. Best of all from the point of view of those who control it and make huge profits from it, it is not hindered by any moral scruple. Modern police officers have a perpetual consciousness of public opinion, a constant awareness that they must proceed by the book. It is inevitable that it should be so: the actions of the guardians of the law must be subject to public scrutiny.

But the drug barons see such things only as weaknesses in the opposing army, as during the course of operations they undoubtedly are. They are unimpeded by ethical considerations; they make sure their own operations are swift and efficient, without any of the lets or hindrance of conscience.

In his comfortable mansion in the Severn Valley, Keith Sugden, the shadowy figure who ultimately controlled the drugs which Matthew Upson and Jamie Lawson had been purveying at the other end of the chain, was swiftly made aware of the details of these deaths.

He felt no sorrow for these infantrymen in his army, whereas policemen would have felt anger when other policemen they did not even know were killed. These deaths were to him an inconvenience on a remote and relatively unimportant front in his war. They were at most an irritation, and that only if the focus of a murder investigation might shed an

116

unwelcome light on this distant part of his operation. These deaths were a security risk, a small problem which must be addressed, no more.

Sugden was consulted, gave his opinion, and did no more. His opinion would be taken into account, would indeed be heavily weighted in this highly autocratic system, but it would be others, further down the chain of command, in more direct touch with the people involved, who would take the decisions. Sugden was coolly professional: he didn't want other killings, with all the attention and the publicity they would arouse, unless they were really necessary. If the people who knew the situation thought deaths essential, they would be conducted swiftly, efficiently and anonymously.

Simon Kennedy, visited at his home on Sunday night by Lambert and Hook, but not so far by any members of the Drugs Squad, was aware of none of these deliberations. As the CID men had suspected, he was a long way from the inner circle of the organisation, making big money, but not taking big decisions. And totally dependent on those above him in the chain of command.

It was one of those men, the one who had read the *Gloucester Citizen* account of the inquest on Matthew Upson behind the closed doors of his Cheltenham base, who made the decision about Kennedy.

Simon was in the Gloucester branch of the dry-cleaning business which was his official front when he got the phone call. He did not recognise the voice on the other end of the line. When he asked for a name, he was not given one. The tone was brisk but not hostile. 'What time do you close?'

'Five thirty. There isn't usually—'

'Make sure it's prompt. I shall arrive at six, and you won't want anyone around then. I shall come in by the back door.'

Simon tried to ask him what the purpose of this visit was, but he realised even as he spoke that the line was dead. It was another half-hour before he wondered how his mysterious visitor knew about a back entrance that was completely invisible from the street.

He was even more disturbed when the man arrived. He saw him coming through the narrow yard at the back of the premises. A slightly built man, whose leanness made him look a little taller than he was. A man with black hair, cut very short but not shaved, with dark, observant eyes, sallow skin and a thin mouth. He wore a dark grey polo-necked shirt, black trousers and black trainers, and he moved silently over the old flagstones to the back door of the shop. There was nothing about him that was colourful; everything seemed functional, efficient, clear-sighted.

He did not knock, nor even hesitate at the door. A lean arm reached out to the handle, a sinewy hand turned it, and the man was within the building, invisible to any curious eyes which might have observed him taking this private route into the place.

Simon Kennedy recognised him. Minter. A professional killer, who earned serious money. Rumour had it that he was on a permanent retainer with the organisation now, but Simon was not high enough in the hierarchy to be sure one way or the other. All he knew was that the man carried with him an air of menace; whether it came from himself or his sinister calling, Simon was not sure.

Minter took Simon in at a glance, then looked round the cramped little store room into which he had stepped. He took in the locked cupboards, the old flagged floor, the cobwebs in the high corners of the disused room, then moved without invitation through the door and into the shop itself at the front of the building. Simon had already taken the precaution of lowering the security blinds over the plate-glass window and locking the front door of the shop, so that any exchange could not be detected by any curious member of the public on the narrow Gloucester street outside.

Minter walked round the perimeter of the room, inspected the narrow staircase which led to the unoccupied upper storey of the shop, pulled out the two upright chairs which stood by the wall and set them one behind the other in front of the counter, in the centre of the floor. He motioned to one of them; only when Kennedy had sat down meekly as he indicated did he station himself on the other chair. He sat astride it, with his arms folded on the back of it, so that his dark, unblinking eyes were no more than three feet from those of the shop's owner.

Throughout this procedure, Minter had spoken not a word. Simon had attempted first a greeting and then one of the meaningless pleasantries with which people establish communication. Neither had received any acknowledgement from this dark intruder, who had come into the place and behaved as if he and not the man now sitting looking into his face was the owner. He had acted, thought Simon with a sudden burst of terror, as if he was preparing himself for one of the swift, anonymous killings which were his means of earning a handsome living.

That was not Minter's purpose here. Not this time. But he knew that uncertainty made people afraid, and it had become a habit with him to foster it whenever he could. He could see sweat upon Kennedy's face; his forehead shone with it, and that gave Minter satisfaction. Not pleasure, that would be too strong a word, but a feeling of efficiency, an assurance that the man was now properly prepared for the message he had to deliver. He knew the sweating man would not be able to stand the silence as they sat looking at each other, so he waited for him to speak, merely to have the satisfaction of interrupting him.

Simon said, 'Look, I think you'd better begin by—'

'You've slipped up, Mr Kennedy. Your masters are not pleased with you.' The volume was low, but the words were clipped, edged with the menace they were meant to carry.

Simon licked his lips. He wanted to use the man's name, to show that he knew who he was and was aware of the work he did. He needed to establish some kind of rapport, but he could not bring himself to do it. 'I think there must be some mistake. I haven't—'

'You shouldn't have killed that student. Jamie Lawson.

119

Your pusher. Acted without authority. Might have embarrassed the whole organisation.'

The actual death of that wretched boy was an embarrassment, no more, Simon noticed. Even murder was no more than that, in this league. Well, the big league was what he'd wanted, when he'd joined: that and the big money that went with it. The cold eyes were watching him, waiting for a reaction. His throat was dry. The words passed over it like barbed wire as he said, 'He was going to talk to that police superintendent, the next morning, you know, and—'

'You don't take decisions like that. Not at your level.' For the first time, contempt edged into the impassive tone. 'If a pusher needs to be eliminated he will be. But not without the order coming from the right level. And the job won't be done by amateurs.'

He spat the word like the vilest obscenity, so that Simon found he wanted to say something to reassure him, to show that he recognised his status as a professional, unemotional killer. And to emphasise that he wasn't the stumbling novice in the criminal world for which he was being taken. But he couldn't get near to the right words. All he could think of to say was, 'I know that. The boy was dangerous to us, a loose cannon. But I wouldn't have—'

'It was a mistake. Your masters don't allow mistakes.'

'It wasn't my mistake. I didn't—'

'The police won't think he topped himself. That was clumsy. A professional could have told you that. A professional wouldn't have used that method.'

'But – but I didn't . . .' The words wouldn't come as Simon's head reeled. In this world, even a denial that he had killed the boy might be taken as weakness, not strength.

And now, when he most wanted to be interrupted, Minter calmly watched him and said nothing, as if he saw into his very soul and enjoyed the tumult there. Simon's racing brain wondered again whether Minter had been sent to kill him, whether he would be swiftly eliminated here, in this quiet shop which was the front for his criminal activities, and his body not discovered until the next morning. There would be an awful irony about the building which had been used to hide the real source of his income being used now to hide his body.

When Minter spoke at last, his ice-cool words cut into Simon's racing thoughts. They brought a kind of reassurance, as if the man had seen these thoughts and been irritated that they should be so far from the mark. 'I'm a messenger today, that's all. That's not my real work, but I'm happy to carry the occasional message.'

Simon forced himself to look for a moment into the dark pupils which seemed to see so much. The man was little older than he was, yet he felt a world of experience away. Simon wanted to assure him that he knew what his real work was, to recognise the standing that a professional killer should have. Instead, he could only stutter, 'Yes, I see. And – and what is your message?'

Minter studied him for a moment. He was as motionless as marble, but Simon could see the vein in his temple, as though it had been carved there as an exercise by a master sculptor. 'You're finished, Mr Kennedy. Get out while you can. Destroy all the evidence that you were ever connected with the trade. That is the message your masters required me to deliver.'

He had spoken throughout of 'your' not 'our' masters, Simon thought inconsequentially. As if he was asserting his position as a man on the outside. A man who sold his services but could not be permanently bought. Successful murder brought its own cache, its own massive self-assurance. Simon said dully, 'But I haven't done anything. It's not my fault that—'

'It's your fault that the police are fishing around at the university. Your fault that your masters are having to close down the operation there.' Minter was suddenly impatient with the naivety of this pretender to criminal rank.

'But – but it wasn't me who killed Jamie Lawson.'

'So you say. It doesn't really matter.' Minter had delivered his message and was anxious to be away. Small talk wasn't his way. Neither was explaining himself or others to the small fry on the edge of the criminal world. He wasn't used to being used as a messenger and he didn't like it. But he knew that the men at the top of the pile would want to know whether Kennedy had accepted this. The man had no alternative, but that didn't seem to have dawned on him yet.

Simon saw himself reduced to penury, flung from his promising position on the ladder of crime to the hard ground beneath. Panic took over as the full implications of this visit belatedly hit him. 'This isn't fair. We're better with Lawson out of the way, anyway. He was a security risk to the operation and—'

'Not your decision. Not even one of your pushers. You should have referred upwards, let the right people decide about things like that.' Patience was a quality not normally required of Minter; it was wearing dangerously thin.

'But I didn't—'

'That's it, then. Find yourself something else to do.' Minter stood up, moved away a little from Kennedy, but did not take his eyes off him. It was a habit of his trade and it stayed with him, even though he knew this man was no danger to him.

'But I can't! My whole lifestyle is dependent on the network I've developed round here. I've been living up to it. There'll be more business next year, once this affair has blown over. We're developing the distribution networks in Cheltenham and Gloucester now. And the new university's going to grow every year – and there's three months before we get busy with the new intake. I can recruit a whole new network of pushers, if that's what's needed. Everyone's going to forget about this little hiccup if we lie low for a while. By October—'

'By October, you'll be history, Kennedy!' It was the first time Minter had raised his voice, and there was a new, unmistakably vicious note in it.

'But you don't understand! Surely I deserve—'

'You deserve nothing, Kennedy. You don't get second chances, in this business.'

Simon knew it was over. But the panic was still upon him, making him foolish, forcing him to make appeals to this unrelenting man, who he knew in any case could not reprieve him, since he was merely a messenger. 'But what am I to do? My whole life for the last three years has been—'

Minter looked round the dingy shop, looked beyond Kennedy to the thin row of suits and dresses in their polythene covers, waiting to be collected by the public. 'Your affair, not mine, chum. Develop your dry-cleaning business, I should think.' He sounded as if he thought that quite a reasonable joke, but he did not smile. That was not his way.

'But they surely can't think . . . Not for a minor—'

'Death is never minor. That is why some people are paid good sums to make sure it's achieved properly.'

Minter turned at the door, and to Simon's inflamed imagination, he had something of the devil about him now. 'Don't even think of endangering the security of the operation, will you? Your death would be much more efficient than Lawson's if you did.'

Simon Kennedy found himself unable to move for long minutes after Minter had left him. The murder of Jamie Lawson, like the earlier one of Matthew Upson, had seemed a logical development at the time, bringing a kind of release for him. He had not reckoned on this reaction from higher up the organisation.

An hour after Minter had concluded his brief and telling visit to Simon Kennedy, Superintendent Lambert and DS Hook joined DI Rushton for an exchange of views at Oldford CID.

The summer sky was darkening quickly as heavy black clouds built in the west. There would be a storm before morning, probably well before midnight. At quarter past seven on a Monday evening the Murder Room was quiet, which was one reason why Lambert had chosen this time. He found himself suddenly exhausted after the drive back from Yorkshire, another reminder of advancing years. One of his great strengths as a young detective had been that he never felt fatigue. He had been renowned for his spartan endurance of all kinds of weather and all kinds of hours; now he moved gingerly, fearful of that sharp stab of pain in his chest which was the reminder of his mortality. His armchair at home and his king-sized double bed seemed suddenly enormously attractive.

Rushton had the results of the post-mortem examination of Jamie Lawson's body. The young man had been garrotted with a rope some ten millimetres in diameter, which had then been attached to a beam to make it look as if he had hanged himself. The angle and nature of the wounds in the neck indicated that he had clearly been dead before he was attached to the beam.

'So he was taken from behind in his own room, presumably by someone who had come there for that specific purpose, since he seems to have brought the rope with him.'

There was silence for a moment as the three of them pictured the scene in that small student room, late on Friday night in an almost residential block. Then, as if to anticipate the inevitable question, Rushton added quietly, 'The few students still resident in the hostel and the site warden have now all been questioned. Not many of them were around on Friday evening, before eleven o'clock: it's a night when most people are out enjoying themselves, not studying in their rooms. No one saw a stranger on Lawson's floor; for that matter, no one saw anyone at all, stranger or friend. The killer chose his time well.'

Lambert sighed. It wasn't surprising. Even when they had visited the student accommodation blocks in broad daylight on Saturday morning, they had carried the air of a site moving from full occupation into vacation. He said, 'You said "he". Can we at least rule out a woman from our suspicions?'

Rushton shook his head. 'It would have been perfectly

possible for a woman to kill by the method used, especially as it seems the boy was taken unawares. And Forensics point out that if the rope was thrown over the beam to haul up the corpse, as the scratches in the dust indicate it was, a woman could have used the leverage to haul the body into the position in which it was found.'

Hook looked at Lambert sharply: he hadn't even considered a woman for the murder. 'You're thinking of Clare Booth?'

Lambert said with a touch of irritation, 'I'm not thinking of anyone. I was just trying to eliminate half the people in the country from the investigation. But all right, Bert, yes. We've not been able to clear Clare Booth of Upson's murder yet, and you felt yourself that the woman was holding something back when we saw her.'

Bert thought of that long-limbed, attractive woman, of her neat cottage, so attractively furnished with antiques, of the handsome Burmese cat, Henry, who had settled on his lap and purred so contentedly. It seemed an unlikely setting for a murderess, for someone who had mercilessly garrotted a hapless student. He said reluctantly, 'Clare Booth knows her way around the university site, I suppose. She'd know when there wouldn't be many students around to see her.'

Rushton pressed four keys on the keyboard of his computer, brought up a different file and a new page of information. 'She's been questioned about her whereabouts on Friday night, like all the others we have in the frame for Upson's murder. She has no satisfactory alibi. She says she was at home watching the telly and reading. There is no one available to confirm that. Apparently a neighbour saw the light on in her sitting room, but she could easily have left it on when she went out.' He turned back to Lambert, pleased to have been able to demonstrate the efficiency of his information storage system.

Hook said, 'But what motive could she possibly have for killing Jamie Lawson?'

'Maybe he knew something about the first murder that she didn't want him to reveal. Perhaps she found out we were

125

going to see him on the following morning and decided she had to shut his mouth.' Rushton looked almost apologetic as he said it, more because of the melodramatic turn of phrase than for the idea itself.

Lambert shook his head wearily. 'We don't even know that the two murders are connected yet. It just seems probable, with so many of the people we have questioned knowing both victims. But we may be looking for two quite separate killers.'

Rushton said, 'I can't think that Lawson's killing isn't connected with drugs. He'd been exposed as a supplier, and you were about to question him in detail on the Saturday morning. Someone stepped in to prevent him talking to you.'

Lambert nodded. 'In the light of the evidence we have, that's certainly the likeliest explanation. All I'm saying is that until we know that for certain, we mustn't close our minds to other possibilities.'

There was often a tension between Bert Hook, who had years ago refused promotion to the rank of inspector and obstinately remained a detective sergeant, and the more orthodox Chris Rushton, who was determined to rise as high as possible in the service. Bert now welcomed the chance to agree with the younger man. 'I can't think that these two killings aren't connected. And if they are, the connection must surely be drugs in some way. Upson was supplying drugs, and making big money from it. One of his pushers was Lawson. I think someone higher up the scale has had both of them killed. Upson for a reason we haven't yet discovered – possibly just rivalry within the organisation, or a feeling he was getting too big for his boots. Lawson because he was likely to tell us stuff they didn't want revealed.'

The three of them were silent, gazing at the almost hypnotic monitor screen of Rushton's computer as it stared its information at them. What Hook had said was perfectly logical, overwhelmingly the most likely scenario. But it depressed them more than any other possible solution. The drugs industry, with its deployment of contract killers to eliminate its victims, was the least likely source to yield them an arrest. The vast majority of unsolved murders in modern Britain are gangland killings, many of them performed coldly and efficiently by these hired hands whose business is swift, anonymous death.

As if he sought to dismiss their gloom by changing the subject, Rushton said, 'What about the man you saw today? This Harold Rees. Were you able to eliminate him from the case?' He pressed more buttons, bringing up the page headed by the ex-miner's name.

Hook looked expectantly at Lambert, who shook his head and said, 'No. Rees remains in the frame. He's the very opposite in most respects of the other possibility we've just been thinking about, the contract killer. Emotional, not planning anything very carefully, but capable of the passionate rage which is the key factor in a lot of killings. Especially if he thought he was protecting or avenging his only daughter.'

Lambert frowned, thinking of his own daughters, of the things he might have done in the heat of passion if he thought they had been wronged, if someone had attacked them, raped them. He would have been more instinctive, more violent in his reaction, even than in defence of his wife, he thought. The father-daughter relationship, growing from when you dandled a tiny, helpless bundle on your knees, defied analysis. It had seemed particularly powerful in Rees. And he had only one daughter.

Lambert felt a need to justify himself with facts, with something more analytical than his thoughts on the man's emotional make-up. So he added, 'On his own admission, Harold Rees was wandering around the area where Matthew Upson was killed for most of the day on which he died. He was in his car and alone for most of that day. He says that Upson failed to meet him in Ledbury, as arranged, and that when he went to the university site, he couldn't find him. But both Charlie Taggart and Jamie Lawson saw Upson at the university on that afternoon. If Rees was as determined to find him as he says he was, it seems odd that he didn't locate him. Rees could well have found him, had some kind of row with him, taken him to the Malverns in his car, and killed him there. He wouldn't have needed a weapon, because we know Upson was killed with his own pistol.'

Hook frowned. He had liked the blunt, clumsy Harold Rees and the family they had visited in that tight little stone house in Yorkshire. But he knew that not all murderers were contemptible. Harold Rees was the kind of man who would commit a single, awful, violent attack in the heat of emotion and perpetrate no other crime in his life. There were several men like that serving lengthy custodial sentences in the prisons of the land. He said, 'But can we connect him with the killing of Jamie Lawson two weeks later?'

Lambert smiled at Hook's earnestness, following his train of thought in wanting to defend that likeable bear of a man they had seen earlier in the day. 'Almost certainly not. But as we agreed earlier, the two deaths may not be directly connected. It's possible that Upson's death merely set off a train of events, probably in the drugs world, which later necessitated the murder of Jamie Lawson.'

Rushton, who had not seen any of the suspects and was thus not entramelled by his own reactions to them, said suddenly, 'What about the girl herself? Kerry Rees.'

Lambert considered this. 'The wronged lover, the girl left pregnant and alone by the man she thought was going to divorce his wife and marry her? I doubt it, in this case. We all know it's happened before, and assuming the murder was committed in the hours after Upson was last seen by Taggart and Jamie Lawson, it's just possible she had the opportunity. She says she was out with friends in the evening, and we've checked that she was: her fellow students confirm that she was with them from seven o'clock onwards.'

He smiled at Rushton, who had turned up just that information on his computer and was surprised that John Lambert, with the wealth of information any case like this threw up, could remember the detail so accurately. 'Kerry Rees could have taken Upson out to the Malverns and killed him and been back with her friends by seven, but it seems highly unlikely. She has a driving licence, but no car of her own. She'd have needed to borrow a vehicle to get him there.'

Rushton said with a little spurt of excitement, 'She could have done it with her father. He was down here all that day with his car, as you said.'

Lambert shook his head. 'She was in an exam that afternoon. And if Harold Rees killed Upson, it was to avenge his daughter, or in a fit of rage at the man's refusal to take her seriously. He wouldn't have involved Kerry in any way in a violent crime: he's far too protective of her.'

Rushton nodded reluctantly. He was loath to accept anything that was based on an assessment of character rather than solid fact, but the chief was far better than he was at assessing such things, and though Lambert would have rejected the idea himself as unscientific, he had a good record of intuitive deduction, when facts were scarce. Chris said, 'What about the wife? She went out of her way to tell us how much she hated her husband.'

Lambert pursed his lips, trying not to sound pedantic as he said, 'She seems to have had nothing but contempt for him – that's not quite the same thing as hatred. But she's in the clear from the time when Upson was last seen by Taggart and Lawson until midnight on that Friday. Unless he wasn't killed until the next day, it seems that we have to rule Liz Upson out. And if she wasn't involved in her husband's killing, it's difficult to connect her with Jamie Lawson's death. There's no evidence that she'd ever met the lad.'

Rushton continued his mental crossing off of possibilities. 'What about the last person to have seen the deceased alive?' He spoke the phrase as if quoting from a manual, and it is true of course that the last person known to have been with a murder victim always arouses police interest and has to be eliminated from suspicion.

'Well, the last person we know of seems to be Jamie Lawson, who's now dead himself. Immediately after Upson had left Charlie Taggart.' Lambert smiled a little at the recollection of the pallid face beneath the black, undisciplined eyebrows, as Taggart struggled with a hangover at the time of their first meeting in the deserted Senior Common Room. 'Nothing to connect Taggart with either of the deaths. Other members of staff have confirmed that he was a friend of Matthew Upson's. He seems to have been just that. Possibly, as he told us, they weren't quite as close in the last couple of years as they'd once been, but no one knows of any serious disagreement between the two of them.'

Rushton stood up and switched on the lights. The room was getting darker as the bank of clouds built outside, heavy and ominous. Resuming his seat, he flashed up the paragraphs of information on Taggart on his monitor screen; the letters glowed brightly in the darkening room. 'Taggart would have known the second victim too, wouldn't he?'

Lambert shook his head. 'He says he was aware of him, but only as a problem student whose name came up in meetings. That sounds about right. He knew that Upson had a meeting arranged with Jamie Lawson on the afternoon of the day when he disappeared, because he saw Upson himself just before that meeting and asked him to go for a drink.'

Rushton nodded. 'An offer which was refused.' He swung round from his screen to face the other two. 'Perhaps if we knew who Upson was off to meet when he refused to go for that drink we'd have our murderer. But I've had extensive enquiries made on the site, and no one else but Taggart and Lawson seems to have seen Upson on that Friday afternoon.'

Hook said, 'I can't see any reason why Taggart should be involved. If he had any connection with the supply of drugs, he'd be well in the frame – perhaps making a bid to take over Upson's lucrative corner of the trade. But he seems to be totally clean, as far as that's concerned.'

Rushton flicked to the second page of his information on Charlie Taggart. 'He's also in the clear for that Friday night when we think Upson was killed. He was playing in an evening cricket match. When Upson refused the offer of a quick drink with him, he went straight off to the cricket club. Helped to mark out the wicket, played in the match, stayed drinking afterwards until the last group broke up at nearly midnight. There's a whole group of his team-mates who confirm that.'

Bert Hook grinned his satisfaction. 'Charlie Taggart can't be a murderer, then, if he's a cricketer. If he was a bloody golfer, he might be up to all kinds of wicked things.'

He glanced sideways at Lambert, who refused to rise to the bait. 'It seems almost impossible that the deaths of Upson and Jamie Lawson aren't connected. And if they are, the connection must surely be drugs. The connection we know of is Simon Kennedy, who certainly knew all about what was going on and is involved in the drugs racket in a big way himself. One rung up the ladder from Upson, it seems. Chris, did you—'

He was interrupted by the sound of a phone, ringing out unnaturally loudly in the evening quiet of the Murder Room. Rushton picked it up and was immediately alert. They heard only his clipped responses. 'Yes. . . . When was this? . . . How long was he there? . . . Did they leave together? . . . No, just stay with him. . . . Use your own judgement on that. Ring in again if there are any further developments.'

He put down the phone, glanced at the figures he had jotted on the pad on front of him, turned back again to face John Lambert. 'That was DC Evans, sir. The tail you asked me to put on Simon Kennedy. Reporting in. Kennedy was at his dry-cleaning shop in Gloucester this evening. On his own. Until he had a visitor, that is. At just after six o'clock.'

He paused, as if he wanted to make the maximum impact with this news, and Lambert rapped impatiently, 'Who, for God's sake?'

'Derek Minter.'

If Rushton had indeed sought to create an effect, he had it. All three of them knew that name, knew that Minter was a contract killer, operating for the tycoons of the criminal world they fought, operating with such cool efficiency that so far there had never been the grounds for an arrest, let alone a charge. Even among these experienced CID men, death carried its own aura, and the name brought a chill into the warm room.

Lambert's first thought was that they had yet a third murder to contend with. 'Has DC Evans seen Kennedy since Minter left?'

'Yes. He left about quarter of an hour after Minter had gone. Looking shaken, Evans said. He's at his home now.'

Outside the building, there was a sudden vivid flash against the purple sky, and a roll of thunder, distant but prolonged, rumbled through the brooding air. The first heavy drops of rain began to thud down on to the parched ground.

Fourteen

On the morning of Tuesday 29 June, Clare Booth woke early after a restless night. The thunder rain which had hammered so hard on the Velux window in the roof last night was over now. She could see white clouds and a patch of blue sky through that window, and the birds sang out their celebrations in the clear, fresh morning air.

Clare lay for a moment looking at the high ceiling of her bedroom. The builder had been right to leave the soaring vaults of the school ceiling as a feature when he converted the old stone building into houses, she thought inconsequentially, even if it made it difficult for decorating. It gave the room character, where modern bedrooms tended to be just one more small box in a boxy house.

Matt had always liked it when they lay here together, looking at that ceiling and chatting quietly, after the high exchanges of passion were spent. Those had been some of the best moments. Matt had been at his best then, too, most relaxed and most happy. She thought of his body, which had once given her so much pleasure, lying now cold as alabaster in its black cupboard in the wall of the mortuary. It would not be released until his murderer was arrested, she knew, and probably not even then. The defending counsel would have a right to a second, independent post-mortem examination, if he wanted to challenge the findings of the original one. Matt's poor body might be torn apart anew, his organs weighed and examined by strangers who had never known that body as a living, moving thing.

She shuddered, but did not move. For ten minutes and more

she lay reviewing their time together, analysing where things had gone wrong. She felt a little resentment still, but none of the wild, unreasoning anger, that wish to hurt and hurt badly, which she had felt on that last, fateful morning.

She knew what she must do today: she had gone over what she planned so often in her mind that it now drummed in her head like some sort of formula. And once she was moving around her neat little cottage, action brought its own kind of release. She even managed to eat and savour a small helping of cereal and a piece of toast. She had thought as she tossed restlessly through the small hours of the night that she would not be able to eat at all.

She knew the girl she wanted to see, knew that she would still be around the university, because she had her final first-year examination to sit on the following day, 30 June. Clare had thought originally that she would contact her at that moment, as she came out of the examination hall. But then she realised that all the students would be on a high as they came out of their last examination. She might not be able to secure the serious hearing she desired; even more important, she wouldn't be able to ensure the privacy she needed, with the girl's fellow students around her, chattering excitedly. And she couldn't afford to start tongues wagging by separating her from her peers in those happy moments of relief from exam stress.

So she must find her today. The snag was that she didn't know where the girl would be, and she didn't want to attract too much notice to herself as she sought her out. She tried the registrar's office first, where she knew all student records were kept. 'Have you any idea of the present whereabouts of Sharon Webster?' she asked. 'She's one of my personal students and I have an urgent message for her.'

The girl behind the desk turned up her computer records, discovered that they hadn't seen Sharon since the beginning of term, offered her the girl's home address in Walsall if Miss Booth wished to forward her message.

'That's all right,' said Clare brightly. 'I have her home

address in my filing cabinet anyway, but I know she's still on site because she's got an exam tomorrow.' She left as swiftly as possible, annoyed with herself that she should have drawn any attention to her quest, even from that moon-faced girl who went back to her coffee and her gossip with every appearance of having dismissed this contact from her mind as soon as it was concluded.

As soon as she entered the Humanities building, Clare spotted one of Sharon's friends, who told her immediately where she would find the girl.

Sharon Webster was where Clare should have sought her at first, in the library. She was an earnest, dutiful girl, with small, thin-rimmed spectacles halfway down a nose that seemed too slender to carry them any higher. She had long, dark straight hair, which fell around her shoulders in a rather undisciplined way, unexpectedly large and beautiful eyes above the spectacles, and a wide, full-lipped mouth. In the year she had spent as one of Clare's small group of personal students she had grown from gawky schoolgirl into something much more attractive. In a year or two she would be a rangily beautiful young woman, in many ways a younger version of Clare herself.

At various times during the past year Clare had found herself having to resist the temptation to take the girl in hand, to deposit her with a good hairdresser, put her in some figure-hugging clothes, and then help her with a discreet application of cosmetics. Sharon Webster could be like one of the stock characters in the old British movies Clare much enjoyed, the librarian who threw away her glasses, let down her hair, smiled a dazzling smile and became suddenly enormously glamorous and the centre of male attention.

But Clare had realised quickly that there was no question of her taking such a personal interest. The girl had a crush on her.

A relatively harmless, transient thing, Clare judged it, a product of a retarded adolescence. At the end of each term tutors held one-to-one sessions with their personal students, to check on their academic progress and discuss any problems. At the first of these, just before Christmas, Sharon had muttered about 'exploring her sexuality'. She had even attempted glances of languorous sensuality from those surprisingly large, soft-grey eyes, and permitted herself a sigh that was intended to convey a wealth of feeling.

Clare had brusquely ignored these signs, concentrated her remarks upon the girl's generally satisfactory academic progress, and dismissed her to her Midlands home with banter about boyfriends and mistletoe.

She had been careful not to be left alone with Sharon throughout the Lent term, and when it had been inevitable that they should be together for the end-of-term assessment of the girl's progress, she had revealed enough of her relationship with Matt Upson to show that her own preferences were resolutely heterosexual. She had not felt she was breaking any confidences with Matt, for their affair was already common knowledge among the staff and the more percipient students.

There had been much sighing from Sharon Webster, and the girl had played the tragic victim of misplaced love around the site a little at the beginning of the summer term, but Clare judged that she was over her breathy infatuation by now. Nevertheless, she thought she could rely on a certain loyalty from the girl, an unquestioning compliance. That was what she needed now.

She stood at the end of one of the island rows of books, studying Sharon Webster carefully, trying to work out if the man sitting four feet to her left was a friend of hers or merely another library-user who was there by chance. The problem was solved as Clare pretended to consult one of the large tomes on the development of the Third Reich. The man she did not know looked at his watch, shut his book, rose and disappeared. He did not take his leave of Sharon Webster.

Clare came out from behind the shelves and stood on the other side of the library table until Sharon looked up The girl was surprised, a startled hamster as she regarded her tutor over the small round lenses. 'I need a word,' whispered Clare. 'Not here. Can we go to my room?'

Sharon nodded, trying not to look apprehensive, wondering what student sin she had committed that she should be summoned thus from her studies. It was less than a hundred yards from the library to Clare Booth's tutorial room, most of it down a wide, deserted corridor. Clare strode ahead of the puzzled girl, anxious that no one should remember seeing them together, that no one would be able to hint at the collusion she was now planning.

Clare shut the door of her room carefully. Now that lectures had finished for the year there were not many tutors around, but she knew she needed to be careful. She made herself sit down, gestured with a forced smile to the chair on the other side of her desk. 'It's nothing much, really,' she lied.

'Is it one of my assignments?' asked Sharon anxiously. 'I think they were all in on time – well, one of them was a day late, but Mr Dempsey said that was all right. I might have—'

'No. No, it's not your work, Sharon. No need for you to be worried on that account. It's – well, it's just something I wanted you to do for me, that's all. Nothing very important.'

The girl's young, vulnerable face flushed pink with pleasure, the glow extending right down to her long, rather elegant neck. 'Anything, Clare. Glad to be of any help!' Most of the younger tutors encouraged students to use first names, and Sharon, coming from a strict girls-only school, had found that difficult at first. Now she produced Clare's name readily, as if she felt for the first time an equal with this woman who had been for so long at the centre of her breathy fantasies. The idea that she could do something to help this loose-limbed, athletic older woman was an enormous, totally unexpected bonus.

'It's nothing much really,' Clare repeated, giving her a quick, nervous smile. She was trying to disguise how important this was to her, and feeling that she was failing completely to do so. 'It's just that – well, it would help me if

I could say I was with you at a particular time.' All the words she had rehearsed so feverishly in the dark hours before the dawn had suddenly gone, and she felt like a foolish girl trying to deceive an experienced adult. Deceit wasn't her thing; she wasn't practised in it, and she was in danger of making an awful mess of this.

Sharon was eager to help, but puzzled. 'When was this? I'm sure there'll be no difficulty.' She brushed a strand of dark hair away from her face and smiled her obedience.

Now it was Sharon who was like a bright child, anxious to please a favoured adult, thought Clare. Suddenly this no longer seemed a good idea, but she couldn't think of any way of turning back now. 'It was quite a while ago now. Nearly three weeks ago – the eleventh of June. A Friday, I think it would be.'

Her attempts at vagueness were triumphantly dismissed. 'The day that Matt Upson disappeared!' said Sharon delightedly, thus pinpointing the very event Clare had hoped that she would miss.

'Was it? Yes, I suppose it was. Well, I'd just like you to tell anyone who asks you about it that you were with me on that morning, that's all. Unless you've any real objection, that is.'

'None at all. I'll be delighted to do anything that helps to repay you for all your care and attention during the year. I couldn't have had a better personal tutor, and—'

'That's all right, then? If anyone asks you, you'll tell them I was with you on that morning?'

'Yes, of course I will. What time, exactly? I mean, when was I with you, and for how long?'

She was making it seem more of a big deal, more of a plot between the two of them, than Clare had envisaged when she had thought of this idea. She wished again that she could drop the whole thing, tell Sharon to go away and forget all about it, but she knew she could not do that now. The girl would be even more intrigued, even more curious, if the drama she had glimpsed was now whisked away.

138

Clare tried to sound offhand as she said, 'Time? Oh, yes, I suppose we should agree on something. Well, suppose you say we met at about ten on that morning, and that our meeting lasted for about an hour.'

'Yes, I see. And what were we talking about? An hour is quite a long time, isn't it?'

'Yes, I suppose it is. Well, let's say we were reviewing your progress for the year, shall we?'

'All right. But would you allot all of your students a full hour for that? That's the kind of question the police are likely to ask, isn't it?'

Clare looked sharply into the eager, attentive face. It was the first time the police had been mentioned. She had intended to avoid all reference to them, to leave it vague whom this story might be intended to deceive. But this girl had seen immediately what she was about. If she was as transparent as that, what chance did she stand against those two experienced and watchful CID men who had come to her cottage five days ago? She tried to quell a panic rising to the back of her throat as she said, 'I suppose you're right. Well, let's say that I was helping you a little with one of your nineteenth-century theme studies. The rise of Bismarck, shall we say?'

'Yes, all right. And his relations with Kaiser Wilhelm, eh? That's fresh enough in my mind, if they want to follow it up.' For a moment, she looked as if she was going to make a note of the topic. Then she just nodded her head several times with satisfaction.

She's enjoying this, thought Clare. She suddenly wanted to be as far as possible from Sharon Webster, to be free of those large, earnest and resolutely loyal grey eyes. 'Well, that's agreed, then. It's a hundred to one that neither the police nor anyone else will ever ask you about that Friday, but if they do, we know what we're both going to tell them. Now, I mustn't keep you from your studies any longer, not with your last exam tomorrow. Very best of luck with that, by the way, though I'm sure you won't need it!'

Sharon glanced automatically at the electric kettle and the

mugs in the corner of the room. She had hoped for a coffee, to savour the moments of tutor and favourite student made intimate by the spirit of collusion, but apparently it was not to be. She wondered what her lovely Clare's connection could be with the death of Matt Upson, that she should think it necessary to concoct this story, but she wouldn't press her further. Rather would she display her unquestioning loyalty to her heroine. Perhaps she might find out more in a few months, when this was all over and the danger to Clare averted. She stood up determinedly and took her leave, resisting the temptation to lay an assuring hand on Clare's arm.

Clare watched the girl striding resolutely away down the corridor, regretting already that she had ever involved her like this. She remembered now why this day, 29 June, had rung a bell in her memory that morning. It was the feast of Saints Peter and Paul. In her childhood, it had been a Holiday of Obligation at her Catholic school, and they had all looked forward to it fervently as a glorious respite from lessons, a day spent in the long summer warmth. Memory said those days were always sunny.

Now all the twenty-ninth meant to her was that it was eighteen days since the murder of Matt Upson. And still no one had come to arrest her. She had surely made herself a little safer this morning.

The hospital was cool, muted, efficient. Everyone seemed to know what they were about. Except the patients. This must be how police stations seemed, thought John Lambert, to those who weren't familiar with their myriad deficiencies, their constant stumblings towards effectiveness.

The ECG operator ran quickly through a simplified version of how the machine worked – too quickly for a bewildered detective superintendent to follow him. Lambert stared stupidly at the wires as they were attached to his chest, obeyed the simple instructions he was given with the concentrated, dutiful application of a child. He stared at the ceiling of the bleak, aseptic room and was pleased to note a few cracks in the plaster at the top of the wall. It was just a room, after all, like other rooms in other places.

He had woken just after midnight with that sharp pain again, right beneath the place where the man now set one of the contacts. He had cried out in his sleep with the suddenness of the stabbing, waking Christine. She had made him promise that he would give all the details, without minimising the severity of the pain, when he was asked about it by the medicos this morning.

He went over the details of how he would phrase it for them in his head, several times, while the contacts were attached to different places and the machine whirred behind him. In the end, he was not given the chance to relay any new details. The ECG operator stripped the clips swiftly away from his chest and back and said simply, 'That's it, then, Mr Lambert. We shall be in contact with your GP with the results and any comments within a few days.'

Lambert thanked him dutifully. He was out of the ECG unit before he fully comprehended what was happening. The pain gave him a sharp stab as he stooped to unlock his car, like a familiar companion reminding him that it was still there.

Liz Upson stood for a moment on the doorstep of her house, looking into the grey, observant eyes of Superintendent John Lambert.

She did not appear to be disconcerted by this visit. All she said was, 'I'm glad you came whilst the children were at school.' Then she lowered her eyes the few inches that were necessary for them to take in an inscrutable Bert Hook and said, 'I suppose you'd better come in.'

They sat down in the neat, clean sitting room, where the only evidence of children was a CD of the latest pop group on top of the hi-fi column in the corner. There were studio photographs of both the children at about the age of five, staring with wide-eyed childish innocence at some object held above the camera. There was no picture of the dead Matthew Upson, no other trace of the husband

and father who had once lived a large part of his life in this room.

Liz Upson moved characteristically on to the attack before they could question her. 'I want to organise Matt's funeral,' she said. 'Get it over and out of the way. It's upsetting for the children, waiting like this. And it must be agony for old Mrs Upson. God knows, I've no reason to be kind to the old bat, but she is his mother, and she must be very upset.'

'I heard you'd been enquiring at the station,' said Lambert calmly. 'I think they explained the situation to you there. There's no way that the body can be released for interment until we have concluded our enquiries. It's upsetting to relatives, I know, but this is the normal situation in a murder case.'

'It's a bloody nuisance. I don't mind for myself, but it's upsetting for the children and anyone else who might want to mourn. We can't begin to get on with the rest of our lives until he's burned and out of our minds.'

Lambert was sure the callousness of the last phrases was deliberate, an act of bravado to challenge their conventional views of how a wife should be reacting. Well, he wouldn't try to shield her feelings, then. 'You can see the point of the system, I'm sure. Cremation is very final, disposing of any evidence which may still lie within the body. It doesn't leave even the option of exhumation, which is still possible after a burial. And I'm sure you wouldn't want us to destroy anything which might help us to convict the person who killed your husband.'

There was a hint of irony in his tone, and she picked it up. 'You know my feelings about Matt, Superintendent. So does Sergeant Hook. I'm not pretending I plan any grieving myself. I just want to close the chapter. The whole book, in fact.' She smiled her satisfaction in the metaphor.

Lambert wondered what new book she planned to open. He could not think that this attractive, fair-haired, intelligent woman planned to remain celibate for very long. For that matter, she might have been conducting an affair or affairs whilst her husband was still alive: she had made no secret of the fact that she regarded her marriage as over. But they had not been able to turn up any close associations, male or female, by discreet CID enquiries. Liz Upson was either without serious entanglements or very careful.

Lambert said, 'We came here about another matter.'

'I hope it won't take long: I'm working this afternoon. I have to change and be out of the house in less than an hour.'

'I wanted to ask you a few questions about the Beretta pistol possessed by your husband. The murder weapon, it now appears.'

She gazed back at him, unperturbed. 'What of it?'

'Your husband did not hold a firearm licence for the pistol.'

She shrugged. 'I'm not surprised. He was never the best organised of men, as you'll perhaps have discovered for yourselves by now. What do you propose to do about it? Charge him posthumously? Or summons the grieving widow? I can't think you'd get a very sympathetic hearing!'

Lambert refused to let her rattle him. 'Do you know how long Matthew had been in possession of the weapon?'

'No. I didn't take any interest in such things. I'm glad it's out of the house for good now, as a matter of fact.'

'It was manufactured in the early eighties. Had he held the weapon since that time?'

Liz Upson considered the matter. Or gave a very good impression of considering it – neither of the watchful, experienced men could be sure which, with this woman. 'He hadn't had it very long. But I couldn't tell you how long. He didn't inform me when he got it, and I've told you before that I'd ceased to take any interest in his actions. He mentioned it one day, that's all, and I remember telling him that I didn't want him showing it off to the children.'

'Had he had it ten years? Five years? Two years?'

'Certainly less than five years. Maybe less than two. Yes,

I'd say he'd held that pistol for two years or something very near that.'

For one who had professed such ignorance, she seemed to be able to place the time of the acquisition of the weapon fairly accurately, in her offhand, throwaway style of delivery. And this timing made sense. Matthew Upson had been making serious money from drugs in the last two years, had without doubt been involved with some very dubious people. He would have had little difficulty acquiring a firearm in such circles, and he might well have felt the need to possess one as some form of insurance. It was ironic that the weapon he had perhaps acquired for personal protection should have been the instrument of his death.

Liz Upson watched impassively as Hook recorded the details in his large, clear hand. Lambert said, 'There's another matter we need to clear up. Your husband's car.'

She flicked her glance from Hook's notebook to Lambert's lined face. 'It's in the garage. Your people have already examined it in considerable detail. But help yourself, if you think it might help.' There was a contemptuous assumption in her tone that it would be a waste of time.

'That won't be necessary. It's the use of the car, rather than the vehicle itself, which is our concern. Would you tell us how your husband got to work on the day when he disappeared, please?'

A flicker of something on that smoothly attractive face: just possibly fear, but more likely merely irritation. 'I've told your officers this already. In detail.'

'Yes. Tell us again, please.' Lambert was as imperturbable as she was. He could keep this up indefinitely, if he thought it would help him. It was a habit of senior CID officers to make people repeat accounts of events they had already given: it was surprising how often people told things differently, a few days later. Sometimes the discrepancies were no more than the result of imperfect recollection; just occasionally, they had real significance, exposing crucial lies.

Liz Upson's account had no such interesting variations.

'Matt's car was in for service on the day he disappeared. I took him to work in my car. I can give you the service bill if you like, dated and receipted.' She allowed herself a little smile of derision.

'That won't be necessary. The story has already been checked with the garage, who confirm it. They told us also that the car was collected by you, not Mr Upson, at the end of the day.'

She sighed. 'That is correct. That is the arrangement we had made. It wasn't convenient for me, but I was used to Matt being a damned nuisance. He said he didn't know when he would get home, so a friend of mine whose children attend the same school ran me down to the garage and I collected it. It's been sitting in the garage ever since.'

'Did your husband say why he thought he might be detained in the university on that day?'

She sighed, with the air of one whose patience was wearing thin. 'He didn't tell me and I didn't ask him. I thought I'd made it abundantly clear at our previous meetings that I'd long since ceased to care what that arsehole was doing.' She threw in the obscenity with due emphasis, and looked automatically at Bert Hook, to whom she had repeatedly used the epithet at their first meeting. He gave her the ghost of a smile and a tiny nod of confirmation.

'So you don't know how he proposed to get home from the university on that Friday?'

'Superintendent, I don't even know *if* he proposed to come home that day. I think he said he'd get a lift from one of his colleagues, but whether that was true or one of his habitual lies I couldn't tell you. You still don't seem to understand that we lived separate lives, for ninety per cent of the time. Our only common interest was the children.'

'So you wouldn't have any idea which particular colleague he might have been hoping would give him a lift? You must see that it's important; we're talking about his final hours in this world. It now seems likely that Matthew was driven to the Malverns by the same person who killed him there shortly afterwards.'

She looked at him steadily. 'I do see that it's important. I'd help you, if I could. I might not be grieving for Matt, but I'd like to see whoever killed him brought to justice. Unfortunately, I can't help you. I've no idea whom Matt was hoping to use as his chauffeur on that Friday. I don't know the people he worked with; I've never even met the majority of them.'

Lambert noticed that she hadn't mentioned Clare Booth as a possibility. She had denied all knowledge of her husband's lovers at their first meeting, but he was sure now that she must have known about the existence of the prolonged affair between her husband and his academic colleague. It seemed almost unnaturally virtuous in her not to be tempted by the chance to throw in a bitchy reference to her husband's lover. But perhaps she remembered her earlier denial of such knowledge: she was a careful woman this, a sturdy opponent. Or perhaps she really was as indifferent to her husband's actions as she had maintained that she was through all their meetings.

He nodded to Hook and they stood up. 'That's all. But please go on thinking about your husband's last day at the university. If you come up with anyone you think he might have been hoping would give him a lift, or indeed anyone he might have been planning to meet, please get in touch with us immediately.'

She nodded. 'I'll certainly think about it. But don't hold your breath. I think if I was going to come up with anything useful, it would almost certainly have occurred to me by now.'

At least she had ended on a conciliatory note, thought Lambert as they went back to the police Mondeo. On the whole, he decided, it was easier to deal with widows who were racked by tears, struggling to come to terms with their loss, than the composed, sometimes almost scornful, Liz Upson.

The lady in question watched them as they climbed a little stiffly into the pool car and drove away. She stood still as a statue beside the window of her house until a minute after the vehicle had disappeared round the corner of her quiet residential road.

Then she went back into the kitchen and dialled a familiar number.

'Can you talk? . . . The police have just been here again. . . . No, the top brass, that Superintendent Lambert and his sidekick. . . . I didn't – just went over old ground that I'd covered before. . . . No, it's my belief they're not much nearer. They're fishing around trying to find out who Matt met in the university on the day of his death, who was going to give him a lift home in the afternoon. . . . Of course I didn't. . . . See you soon – let's make it soon, for God's sake! . . . Yes, all right.'

She put the phone down and stared at it for a moment before she went back to her chores. Before she went upstairs to get dressed for an afternoon at work, she permitted herself a rare, secret smile.

Fifteen

The cafeteria, which was normally crowded at one o'clock, was almost empty today. Many students had finished their exams. Those who hadn't had either run out of money at this late stage of the academic year or were studying at home. The place was about one-tenth full and Sharon Webster was able to enjoy a table to herself.

She propped an open book against a glass of water, but found she could not settle to reading. The excitement of the morning and of Clare Booth's request for assistance were still affecting her too much for that. She watched the good-looking man with a light lunch on his tray pass in front of the counter and exchange a small joke with the cashier as he paid. She was vaguely conscious of seeing him about the site over the last few days. He looked quite personable; he was a little older than her – perhaps a Ph.D. or some other kind of postgraduate student.

She was surprised when he came over and sat at her table, giving her a bright smile of recognition as he did so, but saying nothing. He ate busily for a couple of minutes. Sharon, who was trying not to watch him, had rarely seen plaice, chips and peas disappear so rapidly. She became aware of something quite odd: he had bought not one but two cups of coffee to accompany his meal. She was surprised she had not noticed it when he unloaded the contents of his tray on to the table, but she had been busy ignoring his arrival at the time.

Now, almost in the instant she became aware of the two steaming cups, the puzzle was explained. The man gave her that boyish grin again and slid one of the cups towards her. 'Noticed you only had a glass of water,' he said. 'Thought you might join me for coffee.'

It was the oddest attempt at a pick-up she had met in an admittedly sheltered life. She said coldly, 'I didn't buy one because I didn't want one.' Then, because the severe put-down was not in her nature, she added, 'Thanks all the same.'

'Fair enough!' said the man. But he didn't attempt to take the coffee back. He made short work of a custard tart, licked the ends of his fingers, wiped them on his paper serviette, and said, 'Want anything important, did she, Ms Booth?'

Sharon stared at him, feeling her stomach turn suddenly queasy. 'I don't think that's any of your business, do you?'

'Yes, I do, surprisingly enough. That's exactly what it is, Sharon, my business.' He glanced swiftly round at the scattered customers of the cafeteria, saw that no one was taking any interest in this couple on the periphery, and pushed a card in a small plastic folder under her eyes. It had a photograph of him, staring seriously into the lens, looking even younger than he did here. It told her that he was Detective Constable Mark Whitwell.

Sharon stared first at the card, then back into the friendly face above it. All she could think of to say was, 'How do you know my name? How do you know about Clare?'

'The first is easy. I've been on the site for the last few days, conducting enquiries into a serious crime and keeping my ears open. The first thing I collected was the list of students of a man who was brutally murdered earlier this month.'

'Matt Upson.'

'Precisely. So I knew about you, as well as about thirty other students. You're one of the three who are actually around today, I believe. But I commend your concentration on your revision: you didn't even know that I was working at the same table as you in the library this morning, did you? Hence I was well aware that Clare Booth had called you away for a private word. Which, knowing that Ms Booth had enjoyed what the Sunday papers call a close relationship with the murder victim, made me very curious. Sorry about that, but you do see that it's my job, don't you?'

'I suppose so. But I don't like—'

'So you'll see that I need to know exactly what it was that Ms Booth wanted to talk about so privately.'

'No way. I can't break a confidence, whoever you are.' But even as she tried to be firm, she knew that she was not going to prevail. It was a situation she had never met before, and one in which this smiling, fresh-faced young man seemed to be perfectly at ease.

His smile merely broadened at her denial. Compared with the young, worldly wise toughs he spent much of his time breaking down, this slightly gawky but not unattractive young lady was child's play. 'We can do this down at the station, if you prefer it. But I'd rather not interrupt your revision more than I have to.'

'You bastard! You can't—'

'Fact of life. It's my job to find out things like this. That's what they've paid my last four days' salary for, to roam around the campus and pick up what I can. If you don't talk to me, you'll have to talk to someone. I'll need to report this, you see, and the top brass will come racing out to see you. Lean on you, until you do your citizen's duty and spill the beans. Because it is, you know. Your citizen's duty. Pretentious phrase, but factually true. A man's been killed; no one has the right to retain anything which might be relevant. Sorry, but there it is.' He seemed genuinely apologetic that it should be thus.

'Clare didn't have anything to do with Matt Upson's death! You can be sure of that!' Yet even as she raised her voice so vehemently, an awful doubt crept for the first time into her mind.

'Then the best thing you can do is tell me what she was about this morning. If it proves to have nothing to do with this case, it won't go any further.' He looked around at the students scattered across the wide expanse of polished floor.

One or two had looked across when Sharon raised her voice, but they took it to be no more than a lovers' tiff as he spoke so softly and reassuringly to her.

He seemed almost genuinely sorry to be having to do this to her, thought Sharon. The pig! No wonder other students called them that. She said stiffly, 'I'm sure that it's nothing to do with your precious murder! Clare merely wanted to remind me of a meeting we had a while ago.'

He nodded, made a small, wordless, encouraging noise in his throat, like a dentist encouraging a courageous patient through the discomfort of an extraction. 'And when exactly was this meeting?'

'I don't think I should tell you that.'

'Nevertheless, you're going to, Miss Webster. When?'

'Eighteen days ago. Friday, the eleventh of June.' She could not believe she had been so precise. She was selling out much too easily to this modern Mephistopheles. His smile was like a hypnotist's watch swinging before her blurring vision. She repeated the formula she had agreed an hour before with Clare: 'I was with Miss Booth for an hour. Beginning at about ten o'clock.' They were almost Clare's own words, she thought. They felt like Judas's kiss upon her lips.

Mark Whitwell nodded, as if he was merely confirming what he had known all along. 'But this meeting never took place, did it, Sharon?'

'What do you mean? Of course—'

'Otherwise she'd have had no need to pull you out of the library to arrange the details with you, would she?'

'Well, she just wanted to confirm—'

'She wanted to confirm the details of a meeting which never took place, didn't she?'

'No. Clare wouldn't—'

'Sharon, I'm trying to protect you. I don't think you're a natural lawbreaker. I don't think you realise the trouble you'll get yourself into if you start lying to the police about a serious matter like this. Now, please tell me what really happened this morning.'

She wanted to go on lying, to proceed from a blind loyalty to Clare. But this man's quiet, insistent tones had worn her down. They were going to expose this anyway, the police. Clare had been silly ever to think she could get away with it. 'I agreed with Clare on the details of that meeting. The details that I've just given to you.'

'A meeting which never took place.'

'Well, no. I did meet Clare, because she's my personal tutor, but it wasn't for a full hour, and not at that time.'

'Nor even on that day.'

'No.' Clare was suddenly near to tears, but she felt relief mingling now with her distress.

Mark Whitwell put the fingers of his right hand briefly on the back of hers as it lay on the table. 'You've done the right thing, Sharon. She shouldn't have asked you to lie for her. It was inevitable that it would come out.'

Especially if you were foolish enough to put yourself in the hands of a willing but inexperienced accomplice like Sharon Webster, he thought, as he went away to report his findings.

In the cafeteria, Sharon was staring miserably at an empty coffee cup. She had drunk Mephistopheles' offering after all, without realising it.

The air smelt fresh as a seaside breeze after the rain. The gardener was completing the last broad stripe of his mowing of the long lawn in front of Simon Kennedy's house when Hook parked the Mondeo as quietly as he could on the gravel below the front door and he and Lambert climbed unhurriedly out. The man completed his task, stopped the mower and looked curiously at the two large men, as they surveyed the results of his handiwork in the weedless lawn beds and the borders of annuals that were coming towards full bloom.

Kennedy noticed his gardener's interest. He was standing in the open doorway before the CID men had time to ring the bell. 'It isn't convenient, you know, your coming here like this. People start talking when they see police around.'

Hook allowed his eyebrows to rise in rather hurt surprise. 'We could have done it at the station, Mr Kennedy. Or in one of your dry-cleaning shops, if you'd preferred it. The choice was yours, when I rang.'

'Well, you'd better come in, now you're here.' Kennedy stood for a moment above them on the top step before he turned away, trying to look taller than he was, as if he needed to boost his confidence. He took them into the room to the right of the front door where they had talked on their first visit, watched them as they sat down in the same chairs, with their backs to the light from the window. When they had been here two days previously he had tried to take that position for himself, and been frustrated. This time he did not even attempt the move, as if he recognised that the odds in this strange game of lies he was playing had been subtly changed.

Lambert was unhurried, watching his man without embarrassment, studying the changes in his demeanour from Sunday night. His well-cut dark hair was tousled, and his hand strayed nervously to stroke the earring in his small, well-formed right ear. In his ruffled state, the small, tightly cut triangle of hair on the point of his chin looked even more ridiculous, like a piece of stage make-up applied by an over-ambitious amateur. He was waiting for a question; when it did not come, he could not resist the compulsion to speak. 'I don't know why you're here, anyway. We said all we had to say to each other on Sunday evening.'

Lambert smiled, noting the man's discomfiture, watching it grow in the silence. He looked round the room, with its expensive drapery and furnishings, its tastefully framed prints of British cathedrals, its air of little-used, anonymous opulence. Then he said, 'On the contrary, I think you have a lot more to tell us, Mr Kennedy.'

Simon ran his hand through his hair, trying desperately to find some means of keeping his end up in this contest where he seemed to have so few weapons. He hadn't played it often before. Only now was he realising that you never knew exactly how much the police knew, how much you could give away by some remark which might reveal a fact they did not already possess. He tried not to show any nervousness, then found himself doing the most obvious thing of all: licking his dry lips before he spoke.

But it was necessary: they felt like sandpaper beneath his desperately working tongue as he said, 'I told you on Sunday: I'm a respectable small businessman, becoming larger, making a success from modest beginnings. This amounts to harassment, you know. You seem to think there's something shameful about growing from one shop to three in four years.' He jutted the absurd black-triangled chin at them and said with an attempt at heroic defiance, 'Well, I'm not ashamed of it. I'm not going to apologise for success.'

'And we wouldn't expect you to, would we, DS Hook? Not if that success was achieved by legitimate means.'

They were playing with him. He felt like a bull waiting for the thrusts to come while they indulged in passes. 'I told you, I'm not going to apologise, and you shouldn't be coming here—'

'Come off it, Kennedy.' Lambert's voice was suddenly a whiplash of contempt, startling even Hook in that quiet room. 'We all three know where your money comes from. We all know just where you got the funds to buy this place, to run your Porsche, to pay that gardener out there.'

As if responding to a cue, the worker outside passed close to the window, a hoe over his shoulder, risking a swift, curious glance inward to try to see what was happening between the police officers and his employer.

Kennedy's right hand was fingering the earring again. The left one ran suddenly through his hair, a limb which was running out of control. 'I don't know what you're talking about. Really, if you're going to go on like this, I think I feel inclined to contact my lawyer and—'

'Do that! He'd better be good. Because we're interested

in something even more serious than drugs, Mr Kennedy. Murder. The unlawful killing of Jamie Lawson, student and dealer in ecstasy, cocaine, heroin and amphetamines. Supplied by one Simon Kennedy. Through his middleman, Matthew Upson. Also murdered, two weeks earlier. Reactions, please, Mr Kennedy. Or would you rather do this in the presence of your lawyer?'

Kennedy glanced from one to the other of the two impassive, observant faces, as if seeking some avenue of escape. 'I didn't kill Matthew Upson. I didn't kill Jamie Lawson. You're mad to suggest it! I can account for my whereabouts when they were killed. I'm sure I can.'

Lambert continued to watch him squirming, like a rabbit caught in the glare of those grey eyes, which seemed never to blink. It was Hook who said quietly, 'Maybe you didn't kill him yourself, Mr Kennedy. To those who make their money in the drugs industry, there are other means readily available. Contract killers.'

'I – I don't know what you mean.' But the conviction had drained from his voice even as the colour left his face. Suddenly, he felt he knew what was coming. And he could see no way out of the nightmare in which he was floundering.

Lambert's voice seemed to be coming from a great distance as it said, 'I think you do, Mr Kennedy. You were visited by a known contract killer last night, in the Gloucester branch of your dry-cleaning firm. He arrived at two minutes past six and left twenty minutes later. Why did you summon him, Mr Kennedy? Were you planning his next assignment? Or merely paying the balance due on the last one?'

Simon stared at him, wanting to pinch himself and awake from this, knowing that he could not because it was not dream but reality. He had felt his world collapsing about his ears when Minter had told him that his drug supply days were over. Now it was not bankruptcy and the sale of all he held dear but murder charges which were threatening him. He said hoarsely, 'You've got it all wrong. I didn't summon Derek Minter. He arranged that meeting, not me.'

'For what purpose?'

The thin shoulders rose, then fell helplessly. 'Not killing. And not to be paid for killing. Minter brought me a message, that's all.'

'Really. And what precisely was this message that was brought to you by a man whose business is murder, Mr Kennedy?'

'He – he was warning me not to get involved in the drugs business, that's all.'

Lambert snorted his derision. 'I'm losing patience, Mr Kennedy. Are you going to tell us why Minter visited you, or not?'

'I – I can't! It's too – well, too complicated.'

Lambert said, 'I've had enough of this. Simon Kennedy, I am arresting you on suspicion of the murder of Jamie Lawson. You do not have to say anything, but it may harm your defence if you do not mention when questioned something which you later rely on in court. Anything you do say will be recorded and may be given in evidence.'

'You can't mean to . . . You're making a big mistake.'

'Ask your lawyer about that!'

They stood one on each side of him, like young coppers guarding a man being taken into custody, whilst he told his astonished wife what was happening. Then they led him past his open-mouthed gardener and Lambert sat beside him in grim-faced silence while Hook drove the Mondeo back into Oldford.

When he was safely under lock and key, the custody sergeant, always reluctant about holding people 'on suspicion', said uneasily to Lambert, 'Have we enough to make it stick?'

'Not at the moment. But we can hold him for twenty-four hours. Let's see what a night in the cells does to loosen his tongue.'

Lambert's own words rang in his ears as he drove his old Vauxhall Senator wearily home from the station. They had a rather desperate sound.

156

Sixteen

It was Wednesday 30 June. Nineteen days now since Matt Upson had died, sixteen days since she had reported him missing, nine days since the body had been found, eight days since she had identified it as that of her husband. Liz Upson ticked off the figures, as she had done each day since Matt disappeared. They were a catalogue of her loneliness.

She had read somewhere that most of the murders which were not solved within a week remained unsolved. Perhaps they would never be able to establish who had killed Matt now.

Liz felt very isolated. She had a need for reassurance, a need to know what was going on in this investigation, what kind of progress the police were making. There was no definite sign that they were getting nearer to an arrest. She wondered if she had overdone the obscenities when she had spoken to the police herself. On that first occasion, when she had reported Matt's disappearance to that stolid Sergeant Hook, she had been driven on by a need to shock him out of his complacency, to startle that weather-beaten, decent face into some sort of reaction. She smiled at how he had almost winced when she kept calling her missing husband an 'arsehole' when she was supposed to be conventionally anxious about his disappearance. Well, she couldn't have known he was dead then, could she? She was only reporting him as a missing person. So it wasn't in such bad taste, after all.

After the body had been discovered and the two of them had come to see her, she had found that superintendent fellow, Lambert, more inscrutable. But anyway, she hadn't said anything which wasn't true. Matt was an arsehole of a husband, had become increasingly so in the last years of their marriage.

She would give him a decent funeral, in due course. There was no need to upset the children more than was strictly necessary. She saw herself dressed completely in black, the demure, dignified widow. She would not simulate weeping grief: no need for that sort of hypocrisy. She would be austere but controlled, an isolated icon of mourning, compelling sympathy from the onlookers at church and crematorium by the stoicism with which she was conducting herself through the ordeal.

She had rehearsed this scene often in the last few days. Playing the part would give her great pleasure, and infuriate that bitch of a mother-in-law, who would know her real feelings all the time. And it would put Matt firmly in the past, draw a line under that troubled and mistaken chapter in her life.

Then she would be able to get on with the future, as she longed so heartily to do. That yearning made her feel again how lonely and vulnerable she was, beneath that carapace of contempt she had used to hide herself from the police. It wasn't easy to maintain your composure when the only conversation you had was with two children of eight and ten.

It was a splendid morning, with blue sky and high white clouds, moving fast on a warm south wind. A bracing English day; it was the kind of morning on which she would have loved to feel the wind tossing her hair as she climbed the spine of the Malverns, with her lover at her side. But the thought that she could not do that only made her sense of isolation more acute.

Her loneliness seemed to surround her like a hostile presence, with a life of its own, observant and mocking. At ten thirty on that Wednesday morning, she could stand it no longer. She rang her lover.

She felt a thrill at the sound of his voice, cautious as it was. She spoke quickly, beset by a sudden, irrational fear that he might ring off. 'It's me. Liz. I know we weren't supposed to communicate, but—'

'We weren't, no. We agreed, Liz. It can only bring suspicion that we don't need. The police are floundering about looking for a killer they can't identify. It can only bring suspicion down upon us if they know about us. Upon you, in particular. We agreed, Liz.'

She could picture his anxious, caring face at the other end of the line as he tried to convince her. It made her want to cry out her love for him. Instead, she said, 'I need you. I just want to be touched, reassured, whatever you like. I'm lonely, having only the kids to speak to, avoiding the very mention of Matt all the time.' She realised that she was pleading, when she had meant never to plead again with a man for the rest of her life. But the circumstances were surely extraordinary. Unique, in fact.

Perhaps he caught the note of hysteria that she had been determined he would not hear. He said, 'Where are you ringing from?'

'I'm at home. There's no one around.'

'We can't meet there. Or here, for that matter.'

It was an admission that they were going to meet somewhere, and both of them realised it.

Liz said joyfully, 'Where, then? You suggest a place and a time. You think these things through better than me.' It was true enough, though it sounded like a shameless piece of flattery, and in a less stressful moment he would have teased her about it. She thought for an instant about the many such moments they would have in the future, and the pleasure of the thought almost dissolved her into tears.

She heard him breathing at the other end of the line, almost as if he was beside her. Then he said, 'Tonight. In that park near the centre of Malvern. Where we met once before. As near to dark as possible.'

'Nine thirty? I can't rely on a babysitter for much later than that.'

'All right. Nine thirty it is. By that small lake. There are plenty of benches round there. Sit down somewhere quiet and I'll find you.'

'All right. I can't wait to see you, my darling!'

But he had put the phone down before she got to the endearment.

Clare Booth was marking examination papers. They should have been a distraction from her other problems; students' futures hung on her judgements here, and that normally made concentration easy for her. She was a good tutor, effective in her teaching and highly respected by her students for her integrity. But today she just couldn't settle to her task; she found herself reading the same page of script over and over again. It was almost a relief when the doorbell rang and she saw the dark shapes of Lambert and Hook behind the frosted glass.

They came briskly into the cottage, seeming larger than ever among the delicate antique furniture, scarcely acknowledging her greeting and her invitation to sit down. And there was no ambiguity in Lambert's opening. He said with unusual aggression, 'You probably guessed why we needed to see you this morning. You've been caught out in a lie. A deliberate attempt to pervert the course of our investigation.'

She had thought he was going to say 'to pervert the course of justice'. But that was a legal charge, wasn't it? Perhaps that would come later. For the twentieth time, she regretted the impulsive action she had taken in asking Sharon Webster to help her to deceive them. It wasn't fair to the girl. But she knew she should be thinking about her own position now, not Sharon's. She did not know how to respond to Lambert's accusation, where to begin her defence.

Perhaps Lambert took her silence for denial, for he went on impatiently into an explanation, an assurance that persistence in the lie was useless. 'We have a young detective constable,

Mark Whitwell, operating on the site at the university at the moment. He questioned a student called Sharon Webster yesterday, and found that you had asked her to lie on your behalf.'

Clare said dully, 'I should never have involved Sharon.'

'You should never have involved anyone, Miss Booth. It only concentrates our attention upon the very area you were trying to conceal. Why did you try to set up this clumsy deception?'

Clare thought furiously, desperately trying to cudgel a brain which was refusing to work into some sort of action. In that moment of agonised quiet, Henry, the Burmese cat, strolled unhurriedly across the room, stretched luxuriously, and leapt gracefully onto Bert Hook's ample lap. He nuzzled the knuckles beneath the open notebook, yawned with shut eyes, and set up a purring which sounded unnaturally loud in the heavy silence.

Despite her situation, Clare smiled with an automatic fondness at the mound of luxurious fawn fur. It was Henry and this reaction to him which enabled her to speak, when she had begun to think her tongue was paralysed with fear. 'I was a fool to think I could ever deceive you, wasn't I?'

Lambert was here to ask questions, not answer them. 'Why did you concoct this story? We'll have the truth, please, this time.'

'I – I felt threatened. I was the last person to see Matt alive, wasn't I?'

There was not a flicker on John Lambert's lined, attentive face. No need to give away information when ignorance might be more productive. 'So? Why should you feel the need to lie about it?'

'Well, the last persons to see murder victims are always suspect, aren't they? And I'd already told you that we'd split up – that Matt wasn't going to marry me when I'd been counting on it. And, well, to tell you the truth, we had a hell of a row that last morning. I thought we must have been overheard, that someone was bound to tell you about it. And—'

'And you thought the best solution was to tell a pack of lies. To enlist a young woman to support one of the most ham-fisted attempts at deception that I've come across in years!'

'I panicked! I've sat here for night after night with only Henry to talk to, wondering what was happening, knowing how I'd lied to you when I said I'd last seen Matt on the Wednesday before he disappeared. I felt you must find out at any minute that I'd seen Matt that Friday morning, that I'd been the last one known to have seen him alive.'

He didn't tell her that there'd been other sightings of the dead man, hours later. It was better to keep her on the back foot. 'So you're now telling us that your first lie led to another, more elaborate one. And of course, we have to decide whether we should believe you now about what happened at that last meeting. And if it was indeed the last one.'

Henry was purring more loudly than ever. He stretched his paws, drove his claws a little into Hook's ample thigh, establishing territorial rights. Clare reached a hand towards him, then let it drop helplessly to her side. 'He likes you, Sergeant Hook,' she said inconsequentially.

Bert looked up from his notebook, ignoring the sharp pinpricks in his thigh, feeling the cat's small, warm head respond as he stroked its ears, smiling a little to encourage a belated honesty in the lithe woman who sat opposite him. He said, 'You say you had an argument with Mr Upson on that Friday morning. What was that argument about?'

'I made some remark about a student. Probably a bitchy remark, but I thought he was behaving irresponsibly.'

'Kerry Rees?'

'Yes. You know about her?'

Hook gave her the briefest nod; probably by now they knew more than she did.

'Well, I suppose it wasn't just pastoral care which prompted me. I was as jealous as hell, as I realised once I'd raised the matter. Matt told me it was no longer any of my business what he did, and I flew off the handle. I yelled at him

162

about the way he'd treated me, and he ended up by shouting back at me.'

'Where did this take place?'

'In my tutorial room. I checked afterwards that there was no one in the room on either side of mine, because I was embarrassed, but I thought someone must have heard, even much further away than that. It was quite a row we had.'

Lambert nodded. He did not tell her whether they had already known about this or not. In fact, either no one had heard the altercation, or whoever had heard it had chosen to remain silent about it, probably out of loyalty to this feisty woman with her rangy, athletic body and her attractive, intense face. All their enquiries had thrown up was that she was very popular with her colleagues, who had thought her worthy of someone better than Matthew Upson. He said, 'What time was it when this argument took place?'

'About half-past nine, or perhaps just a little after that. Matt stormed out of my room before ten.' She looked shamefaced again. 'That's why I asked Sharon to say she was with me between ten and eleven. So that people wouldn't think it was me who had taken Matt off to kill him.'

'What makes you so sure that someone "took him off to kill him", Miss Booth? You're suggesting someone took him out to the Malverns in a car and killed him there, I presume.' Lambert was quiet but incisive, a surgeon lifting skin with a scalpel.

'Yes. Isn't that what happened?'

The grey eyes stared hard into hers. 'We think it is, yes. But we have never made that information public.'

Her dark eyes widened a little as the implication hit her. 'Matt must have said . . . Yes, I remember now that he said at the opening of our conversation that he'd been dropped off that day, because his car was in for servicing.'

Lambert paused a little, waiting to see if she would go on, give more detail, make the explanation more elaborate, and less convincing. They often did, when they were lying to get off the hook. Then he said, 'I hope you're now telling us

163

the truth. If you are, you were very foolish to try to set up that deception with Miss Webster. The evidence against you is strong, but at present only circumstantial. We shall need more than that, if we are going to arrest and convict you. But we shall find that evidence, if it exists.'

He stood up, and Bert Hook detached himself with some difficulty from Henry and stood beside him. Clare realised that the tall man's last words had been both a reassurance and a threat.

Perhaps that is exactly what he had intended, she thought, as she watched the police car edge out of the courtyard behind the little row of stone cottages.

Seventeen

C lare Booth would have been less convinced of police omniscience if she had heard John Lambert at Oldford CID an hour later.

He looked and sounded tired, even gloomy, as he spoke to Rushton, Hook and other officers who had been gathering material in the investigation. 'I don't think we're going to find a lot that is new at this stage. The trail is getting colder with each passing day. Scene of Crime and Forensics have given us all they can and aren't likely to come up with anything dramatic at this stage.'

Rushton nodded. 'There's only a dribble of information coming in now. Nothing which seems very significant, really, since we found out that Harold Rees was in the area for most of the day on which Upson died.' He tried – and failed – to avoid looking smug as he allowed them to recall that it was him who had brought Harold Rees to their notice as a suspect.

Perhaps it was because he looked too much like a cat with the cream that Bert Hook felt compelled to point out, 'There's no way that we can connect Rees with the murder of Jamie Lawson. Unless we assume that the two murders aren't connected, that lets him out for the first one too.'

Lambert said, 'We still haven't found any definite connection between the two killings. Perhaps they are quite separate crimes, with different motives and personnel.'

DC Mark Whitwell was pleased to be involved in the deliberations of the hierarchy, to feel that his own views might be asked for and heeded. It emboldened him to say,

'Having roamed around that campus for nearly a week and got the feel of the place, I must say that I'm sure the two killings are connected in some way. It would be a remarkable coincidence, to have murders of two people from the same university campus, both involved in illegal drugs, and to find that there wasn't a connection. Especially as we know that Jamie Lawson was taught by Matthew Upson and was working for him as a pusher. Surely the likeliest thing is that it's one of the drugs barons who's ordered both killings. If they were carried out by a contract killer, that would explain why we don't seem to be getting any closer.'

Lambert nodded slowly, seeing the logic but reluctant to accept Whitwell's conclusion, which would make an arrest much less probable. 'Everything points that way, I agree, and Matthew Upson's death has many of the marks of a contract killing: a shooting, miles from anywhere, with no sign of a weapon and the body not found until well after the event. But there are things about Jamie Lawson's death which are too elaborate for a contract killer. The bullet through the head is far more usual than hanging as a method, for a start. And most contract killers are swift and anonymous: they'd regard the rather clumsy attempt which was made to simulate suicide in Lawson's case as an unnecessary, amateurish diversion, a pointless risk, because they normally leave the scene of any killing as swiftly as possible. They don't care that it looks like murder from the start, so long as they leave nothing of themselves at the scene.'

Rushton nodded. 'I agree with that. But I still think we'll find that the two deaths are connected.'

Lambert shook his head like a man plagued by a persistent fly. 'There's something here which is escaping us, I'm sure. Some simple little thing that we've missed. Maybe some lie or deception from someone which we've accepted a little too easily, because it seemed logical at the time. The only connection we have between the two deaths at the moment is the drugs one, and I agree it's the likeliest link. But it's not the only possible one. Let's all go over all the facts of the case in our own minds and try to see whether we have indeed accepted something too readily, something which has perhaps thrown us off course in the rest of our thinking. Unless anything new comes up today, we'll meet first thing in the morning and see if we have any new thoughts.'

He wondered as he went out to his car whether this sounded to his colleagues like a counsel of despair from a superintendent who was feeling baffled.

In the small, neat stone house in Ossett, Kerry Rees was fretting. She had recognised from the start that her pregnancy was going to change her life. She had only just begun to realise quite how radical those changes were going to be.

She had already suspended for a year the course she had been so much enjoying at the University of Gloucestershire. Now she had been forced to relinquish the holiday job she had secured for herself at the local supermarket. Her mother had found her lifting cartons containing tins of baked beans when she came into the store to buy the family's weekly order, and been appalled. Kerry had played down the danger, but in truth had found herself increasingly tired at the end of the days of steady manual labour. At the end of a week she had acceded to her parents' views that she should give up the work, and been secretly glad to do so.

Now she was confined to walks, reading and helping her mother about the house. She didn't mind that at all, but there were limits to what you could do in a small terraced house. She decided to clean her father's den whilst he was out at the working men's club playing snooker.

His absence would give her a good two hours without interruption, and she knew the place needed tidying and vacuuming. Her mother was forbidden to go into this small cell of male monopoly in the house, but Kerry knew her indulgent father would not take offence if she cleaned it. He would grumble in general terms about women and tidiness, but he was far too fond of Kerry to take any real offence at her efforts.

She stood for a moment just inside the door of the small room, savouring the strangeness of it, feeling the thrill of the illicit in her entry into a male preserve. It was really no more than a small third bedroom, but it had been given to her father as his own when they came here after his enforced retirement from the mine. He would have scorned to call it a study: that was a middle-class word, not for the likes of stern toilers at the coalface like Harold Rees. For a long time, it had just been his room, but he had finally accepted the term 'den' which his wife had bestowed on the place from the start.

It was a room crowded with her father's knick-knacks, things which Kerry's mother had eagerly banished from the rest of the house and her father had been perfectly happy to accommodate here. There were trophies for darts and snooker, small cups which her father had set proud and polished on the small mantelpiece, over the fireplace which had never been used since they came here. There was a faded black and white photograph of her father in a miners' football team, powerful men sitting with their muscular arms folded, staring at the camera as if they thought smiles might be a sign of weakness. She looked fondly for a moment at <u>his</u> father in his 1964 prime, with a shock of jet-black hair cut very short at the sides and a health which seemed to leap out at her even from that dingy picture.

Kerry lifted each of the trophies in turn and dusted the narrow shelf beneath them. He was captain of the Veterans' snooker team at the club now; perhaps at the end of the year there might be another trophy to add to the collection. She vacuumed the floor, moving her father's upright chair away from the desk to allow her to get at the carpet. In truth, Harold Rees didn't need the desk very much; he had little occasion to write, apart from his infrequent letters to his sisters in Wales – he held obstinately to the old-fashioned view that a letter was better than a phone call, because it took more of his time and trouble.

His daughter took a full minute over her dusting of the desktop, still savouring with a small girl's relish the feeling of being in a room which she would not normally have been allowed to penetrate. There were a few paper clips which her father, never one for waste, had detached from official letters, and four ball-pens on the desk. Kerry opened the wide, shallow top drawer of the desk to put them away and leave the surface clear for dusting.

It was then that she saw the letter.

It had the familiar logo of the University of Gloucestershire at its head. That, she decided later, was what made her pick it up and read it. That and the signature of Matt Upson at the bottom of the page. She realised wryly that she had never actually seen that signature before: Matt had been far too wily to commit himself to paper in their short relationship.

She could no more have put it down unread than torn away her hands. It read:

Dear Mr Rees,

Thank you for your letter of 1st June.

I am sorry that you feel the way you do about the situation. In my view it is unfortunate, but by no means as desperate as you seem to feel. It would not have occurred if your daughter had taken the elementary precaution of putting herself on the pill before venturing upon sexual encounters.

Despite what you say, students are adults from the day when they reach the age of eighteen, and are expected to behave as such. The obvious solution to the problem is a termination. I have offered to finance this and to make all the necessary arrangements. Your daughter has seen fit to reject this suggestion.

I am still prepared to finance this simple and safe solution, if you can persuade Kerry to change her mind and behave sensibly; that would enable her to continue her course here without interruption. It is much the most sensible way out of her difficulties, for I am happy to say that she is a gifted and diligent student, who should in due course obtain an excellent degree.

I cannot accede to your suggestion of a meeting. It would in my view serve no useful purpose, since the situation is the one I have set out above.

Yours sincerely,

Matthew Upson

The words swam before Kerry's eyes. She sat down heavily on the chair she had moved, then read them again. Even now, with her eyes fully open, she found the formal, uncompromising tone shocking, from the man who had whispered endearments into her ears.

But it was not Matt Upson's phrases but her father's reaction to them which concerned her now. She read the last sentence several times, hoping it would change its meaning, knowing all the time that it wouldn't.

Her father hadn't had a meeting with Matt arranged, as he had claimed to her and to the police.

He had driven down there to seek Matt out and kill him.

Lambert was in his office, going over the evidence again, trying to isolate the one statement which did not ring true, striving desperately to find the one significant thing they might all have overlooked, when the call was put through to him.

He thought when the phone rang that it must be something connected with the case. It took him a moment to refocus his attention on to what the cool, businesslike female voice at the other end of the line was saying. 'It's the Oldford Medical Centre here, Mr Lambert. Dr Cooper would like a word with you, if it's convenient.'

For a moment he could not place the name. Then he remembered that Dr Cooper was his GP; it was so long since he had seen him that he had almost forgotten the name. He said, 'Yes, it's convenient. I'm on my own at the moment.'

The efficient, unemotional female voice, so used to speaking into the mouthpiece all day, said, 'Hold the line for a moment, please. Dr Cooper will be with you shortly.'

He could picture Cooper now: perhaps ten years older than he was, grey-haired, avuncular, comfortably padded, with an old-fashioned GP's panache. This must be about the results of the ECG test at the hospital. But this call wasn't from the young girl who looked scarcely old enough to be a doctor who had sent him there. This was his own GP. Perhaps that was the protocol in these matters.

Or perhaps they thought it only right to let the older man convey bad news. News that he needed serious surgery! Worse news than that, perhaps – that surgery was useless in his case. That his heart was paying the penalty for all those years of smoking and junk food taken at irregular intervals. That he must retire now and live like an invalid. That he couldn't expect to live for very long. That he should prepare himself for the worst! That death might come at any time!

He could hear the sounds of papers being shifted in the background when the phone crackled again in his ear. Then a deep, gravelly voice said, 'John Lambert? The results of your ECG are through from the hospital. Sorry to trouble you at work, but I thought you'd like to know as soon as possible.'

'Yes, thank you. Very thoughtful of you.' Lambert found his mouth suddenly very dry. Why didn't the old fool tell him and get it over with, instead of trying to break things gently?

'Well, there's nothing wrong with your heart. Nothing wrong at all . . . Mr Lambert, are you still there?'

He was. He was staring dumbly into the mouthpiece of his phone, trying to get words from a tongue which seemed suddenly atrophied. 'Th – thank you, Doctor. You're sure there's nothing wrong, then?'

A chuckle at the other end of the phone, from a man who was delighted to be giving good news. 'Nothing at all. And you don't have to trust an old fool like me: ECGs are quite objective, you know! Designed to show any irregularities in the way the heart is functioning.'

'Yes, I'm sorry.' Lambert took a great, silent breath of

deliverance and managed to resume in his normal voice. 'Well, that's a relief, I must say. I wasn't really worried, of course, but I suppose one is bound to get a little anxious. At the back of one's mind, you know.'

Another chuckle. 'Yes, one is. Bound to get a little anxious, I mean. Well, as I say, there's nothing seriously wrong with your heart.'

Lambert was suddenly fearful Cooper might ring off. 'What do you think it might be, then? I'm sure it's not indigestion, I've never suffered from that.'

Another chuckle. Dr Cooper seemed to find his non-serious predicament quite amusing. 'I don't do diagnoses over the phone. You should come in and see me. But in my view the most likely explanation is a touch of fibrositis – inflammation of muscle tissue. Do you get it when you've been in one position for long periods? Or when you make a sudden movement?'

Lambert found he could suddenly think quite clearly about what was now a minor problem. 'Yes. Both of those. It feels like a severe attack of cramp, in the chest.'

'That's the fellow. Get a touch of it myself at times. More in the neck than the chest, in my case. Pop in to see me, when you've got the time. Give you a few exercises and a prescription for some gunge to rub on it. Must go.'

'Yes. Yes, thank you very much for ringing me so promptly, Doctor.'

He stood up, looked out into the deserted corridor, and shut the door carefully. Then he allowed himself a schoolboy shout of triumph and punched the air so exultantly that his knuckles touched the ceiling.

Only fibrositis! How wives would insist on fussing over nothing. He'd known all along that there was nothing serious.

Bert Hook had never been a great theatre-goer. Few policemen are. But this time it was he who had booked the tickets, he who had assured a rather doubtful Eleanor that she would enjoy the performance.

Eventually, she had silenced her doubts and brought her mother in to babysit their boisterous boys, who felt they were quite old enough to be left on their own but weren't. Bert would never have wanted to see *Hamlet* before he had done his Open University degree, but that didn't mean this wasn't a worthwhile expedition. In any case, she got out so little these days that any evening at the theatre was to be savoured. Eleanor dug out the posh frock and the intelligent expression, put on her face, and sallied forth to a night at the theatre.

She was surprised how much she enjoyed the play. The acoustics of the splendidly restored Festival Theatre at Malvern were good, and the familiar, proverbial phrases came floating up to her with great clarity. The Hamlet was short and stout, not at all the image she had carried from the picture on her classroom wall at school of a young John Gielgud, but she soon forgot her reservations as she watched the actor's intelligent, intense delivery. The only embarrassing moment came when Bert leaned close to her ear and said in a highly audible whisper, 'They've cut out Fortinbras altogether!' which caused a flurry of turning heads and scandalised looks from the row in front.

Even without the warlike Fortinbras, *Hamlet* is a long play, and the interval came quite late in the evening. There was such a long queue for drinks that Eleanor suggested they walk outside for a little while instead, and enjoy the twilight of a splendid day. Bert readily acceded, glad of the opportunity to stretch his legs after two hours of confinement. They went down the broad flight of steps which set off the rear of the theatre so impressively and into the park below, where the soft amber light of the Victorian lamps switched on as they arrived, providing an agreeable glow through the trees and making it seem a little darker than it actually was.

While Bert explained to a secretly amused Eleanor what a perfect example of the Oedipus complex Shakespeare had set out in the character of Hamlet, three hundred years before Freud, they strolled through the still warm half-light and dropped down through the trees to the small ornamental lake. They were on the bridge which spanned its still waters, with the dark mass of the Malverns dramatically outlined above them, when they heard the distant, insistent shrilling of the theatre bell, telling its patrons that the second half of the performance would begin in five minutes.

It was as they turned to complete the circuit of the lake and climb the path back to the theatre that they passed a couple sitting on one of the benches beneath the tallest of the trees. The man made a sudden movement as they approached, embracing the woman, putting his face above hers to kiss her. She seemed at first startled by the movement, which obscured both her face and the man's from the passing couple, but then she responded, putting her arms round the broad shoulders, sliding her hand into her partner's dark hair and holding his head against hers.

The man's move had been swift, and effective in its purpose. But it had come an instant too late. Bert Hook's observant policeman's eyes had recognised the man as Charlie Taggart and the woman as Liz Upson.

Eighteen

In the bright morning light through the living-room window, Kerry Rees stood her ground and glared back at her furious father. But she held on to the back of an upright chair, for she felt her knees trembling as he shouted at her.

'You had no right to be in the room! And certainly no right to be reading my bloody letters!'

She had heard him swear often enough before, but never at her. She tried to keep her voice steady as she said, 'This is more important than manners, Dad, and you know it! I cleaned the room to help Mum, and because I wanted to please you. I found the letter by accident. You couldn't expect me not to read it, when I saw the University of Gloucestershire logo on it!'

'You shouldn't have read it!' His voice rose to a shout of frustration as he repeated himself. She could see his brow like thunder, feel the set of his mind behind it, refusing to consider any argument from her.

'Well, I did read it, Dad! And it told me that you never had any meeting arranged with Matt. In fact, it told me that he had refused to meet you! Did you find him, that day when you drove down there, Dad? Found him and killed him, did you?'

Suddenly, when she had least expected it, she was in tears, sobbing uncontrollably, full of grief, not for the dead man but for the clumsy, loving, helpless father who had killed him, who stood before her now roaring like a captive bear.

It was her tears which broke the tension which had held them apart like a rod of steel. Before either of them knew it, he was at her side, his huge arm round her shoulders, her face against his chest, his throat muttering the wordless comfortings he had used when she was an infant upon his knee. Gradually her shoulders moved less violently and she gained a measure of control over her breathing. Finally she turned her tear-wet face up towards those heavy features she knew so well. There was still a huge gasp in the middle of her question as she said, 'Oh, Dad, why did you do it?'

'I didn't, girl! God knows I'd have liked to, but I didn't. There's phones, you know, as well as letters! I may not like 'em much, but I use 'em, when I 'ave to, don't I? I rang lover boy up, as soon as I got that poncy letter. Told him I was coming down, didn't I? Told him he was going to see me, whether he wanted to or not. That I'd make sure I saw his boss, if he didn't meet me! That's when he said he'd meet me in that pub! Which he never did, God rot his soul!'

Kerry Rees looked up into that face so full of experience and love and believed him. She began to laugh, and went on uncontrollably until her father smiled, and shook her like a doll to stop her.

John Lambert was already in the Murder Room, looking over DI Rushton's shoulder at his computer monitor, when DS Hook arrived in Oldford CID at eight thirty on Thursday 1 July.

Perhaps, Hook thought, twenty days after Upson had gone missing, ten days after the discovery of his body, he had the breakthrough which had seemed so elusive even twelve hours earlier. Or perhaps he was bringing nothing of any significance: he reminded himself as he had done throughout the night that seeing Taggart with Liz Upson could either mean nothing at all or be the missing piece of the picture they had been seeking.

He gave them the new piece of information, the piece which might be the missing one in the jigsaw, or merely part of another and quite different picture. He watched their minds clicking over, digesting this new piece of information,

fitting it in with what they already new. It moved Charlie
Taggart from a cheerful observer on the fringe of things to
a central part in the drama, from a man who had provided
them with a little dispassionate information about the dead
man and his associates to a lover of Upson's widow.

And for John Lambert, who had obeyed until far into the
night his own injunction to examine everything they had
previously accepted about this case, it had an immediate significance. 'They've deliberately concealed their relationship
from all of us, these two,' he said. 'That suggests they definitely had some reason for that. A sinister reason, I think, not
just one of social embarrassment. Many a widow might like
to conceal an affair she had been conducting at the time of her
husband's death, merely because it seemed suddenly in very
bad taste, but Liz Upson wouldn't be one of them. She made
no bones about her contempt for her husband. She wouldn't
have thought it worthwhile concealing a lover. Unless she
had some particular reason to do so. Some reason connected
with her husband's disappearance and eventual death.'

'They were certainly anxious not to be seen last night,' said
Hook. 'Taggart was just an instant too late in seeing me. If
he'd moved into his clinch a second earlier, I wouldn't have
recognised either of them.'

Rushton said, 'I'd be pretty certain this is the first time
they've been together since Upson died. We had a tail on
Liz Upson for six days after the body was found, in view
of the opinions she had expressed about her husband. She
didn't meet anyone involved in the case during that time.'

Lambert smiled ruefully. It was he who had authorised the
observation of Liz Upson, and he who had ordered that it
be discontinued after six days, on the grounds of economy:
surveillance was always the most expensive item in any CID
budget. 'Good thing we had that old fox Bert Hook in our
team, then! Never off duty, someone like Bert!'

Hook made his protestations about this being merely an
extraordinary piece of luck when he was out for an evening
at the theatre, but Rushton as usual wasn't sure how far these

two old sweats were pulling his leg. 'It may be no more than an affair between the two of them that we didn't know about. I can see why she wouldn't want to go public on it, in the days after her husband was found shot. I can't see any immediate connection between this liaison and either of the murders.'

Lambert glanced sharply at him. 'Can't you? You should be able to see a possible one, if you do what I suggested last night and review all our information with sceptical eyes.'

Lambert did not go any further, and Rushton was too proud to ask him where exactly he should look. When the superintendent turned enigmatic, Chris preferred to solve the puzzle for himself rather than ask for the solution.

And there was no doubt that Lambert was excited. There was a new glint in his eye, a new urgency in his voice, as he said to Mark Whitwell, 'Get back to the university campus and watch Charlie Taggart. Drop anything else you were following up and just keep your eye on what Taggart's doing. He hasn't spotted you, has he?'

'No, I don't think so. I haven't even been close to him. I've been mingling with the students, picking up what I could about the drugs scene on the campus. He doesn't seem to be connected with that.'

'Does he know your car?'

'No. Unless he's a lot cleverer than I think he is, he hasn't even realised that I'm on the campus.'

Lambert shook his head. 'I doubt that. But he was probably perfectly happy to see you there, so long as he heard that you were following up the drugs situation. Go back there and watch him like a hawk, then. If he leaves the campus, let us know. And follow him.'

Lambert stayed with Rushton and Hook. With a face like thunder, he went over what he saw as the key facts in the story, the crucial flaws in the evidence which they had used to set up the framework of their enquiries. Chris Rushton, who prided himself on the meticulous checking and documentation of the masses of information gathered in a murder investigation, was appalled that he could have accepted things at face value so glibly. 'We were all so certain that drugs were behind these killings. It seemed the only real connection between the two murders,' he said dully, as if trying to convince himself that anyone else would have followed the same path.

But Rushton was not more appalled than Superintendent John Lambert, who went over and over the facts and tortured himself with the thought of how he might have saved the loss of a young life if he had seen things more clearly a week earlier.

Within twenty minutes, Mark Whitwell radioed in to say that Charles Taggart was indeed on the site at the University of Gloucestershire. At ten fifty, he reported that Taggart had left the campus and that he was following the lecturer. Ten minutes later, his radio voice came through a lot of interference from the steeply rising ridge of the Malvern Hills on his right to say that he had crossed the border into Herefordshire, that there was every sign that Taggart was heading towards the house of Liz Upson.

Lambert and Hook were in the car and through the gates of the police car park at Oldford within thirty seconds. Lambert, still grim-faced as a Soviet statue, said nothing, and Hook, driving swiftly but with due care, had more sense than to try to lessen the strain by speaking himself. Each man spent a tense journey asking himself how he could have been so stupid as to accept things so easily.

They were within half a mile of their destination when Lambert growled, 'They fulfilled the first rule of deception: set your one significant lie amidst as much truth as possible if you want to slide it through.'

Mark Whitwell was parked at the end of the cul de sac where Liz Upson lived. His grey Mondeo was behind a maroon Jaguar, but its wheels were turned sharply outwards, in case he needed to fling his car sideways across the narrow road to prevent an exit by the man he had followed here. He appeared to be reading a newspaper, but they knew by the merest inclination of his head that he was aware of their arrival here. 'Good lad, that!' said Bert, without looking sideways at the DC. They were the first words he had spoken since Lambert had tersely outlined their omissions at Oldford CID.

The whole road was ablaze with the brilliant July flush of roses. Around the big front window of Liz Upson's detached house, the full pink blooms of 'Albertine' blazed in innocent profusion across the brickwork, reaching up exuberantly towards the smaller windows of the bedrooms and the eaves above them.

Taggart's MG sports car was parked in the drive. As they walked up the path, they saw the faces of Liz Upson and Charlie Taggart white with surprise and apprehension amidst the myriad pink roses which danced around the window. It was a strange framework for murderers, thought Bert.

When Liz Upson opened the door to them, Taggart was in the shadows at the back of the hall, as if he had been bent on flight through the rear of the house and then realised the futility of it. When Lambert snapped out, 'You had much better come in here, Charlie Taggart!' he turned, like a rangy dog that had been caught in an act of mischief, and moved hopelessly back into the room where they had glimpsed him at the window with his mistress.

Lambert had decided in the taut silence of the car how he would play this. They would pin these two down with evidence in the next few days, however much they squirmed; he was confident of that. But it would make things much simpler if he could get them to admit the guilt and the detail out of their own mouths. With luck, they would assume he already held more than he had in the way of proof.

Taggart at least looked like a man who knew the game was up. His dark eyes flashed a quick glance at them as they came into the full light of the bright room, then dropped to the carpet and remained there. The bushy, unruly eyebrows almost met across his brow as he strove unsuccessfully to become inscrutable.

If Liz Upson knew this was to be the end, she gave no initial sign of it. She sat down upon the sofa, pulling the tall Taggart down beside her, then made a play of settling back into its comfortable depths. 'To what do we owe the pleasure of this latest visit, gentlemen?' she said. 'I cannot think this is a social call, but I shall do the honours with the coffee whenever you demand it.'

She managed an ironic smile, which she transferred from Lambert to Hook when she got no reaction from the superintendent. But this smile had not the confident condescension of her earlier ones, when she had mocked convention with her contemptuous dismissal of her newly dead husband.

Lambert controlled the anger which suddenly surged through him. This woman had had the better of him and his colleagues for far too long. He said coldly, 'We're here because we've seen through your lies at last. Yours and those of the man sitting beside you!'

She was cool, even now, when she must surely know it was almost over. Charlie Taggart's mobile features had finally frozen into immobility with Lambert's accusation, but she managed a shrug and an appropriate snigger as she said, 'Really, you shouldn't be so easily shocked, Mr Lambert! I made no bones from the first time I saw your sergeant here that I had no use for my husband, and no affection for him either. If Charlie and I chose to conceal our little affair from you, that's our business, surely. It had nothing to do with Matt's death.' She reached her hand out and put it on the wrist of the man beside her, looked into his face with a quick smile of affection, as though by her touch she could inject into his body some of her own composure and bravado.

'Your little affair, as you call it, had everything to do with your husband's death. Without it, that murder might never have happened. A joint enterprise, as were your attempts to conceal it!'

Lambert switched his gaze from the bold woman to the man struggling for control beside her. Taggart clutched her hand as it lay upon his wrist, grasped it indeed so hard that she winced a little with the force of his grip. He found his voice at last, but it rang unnaturally high as he said, 'This is preposterous! I might not have told you about me and Liz, but surely you can understand that we didn't want to start all the tongues wagging, with Matt gone missing. I've given you all the help I could from the start! That first day, when you came in to the university looking for information, I was the only one around to help you. Without me, you'd never have got started so quickly! Without me, you'd never have known – well, lots of things about Matt!'

He threw the last phrase at them with a kind of desperate vagueness. Having found his voice at last, he had gone on for too long, expecting to be interrupted, feeling his words whirling out of control as he became more and more aware of the attention in those intense grey eyes and that long, lined face.

When he was sure that Taggart was not going to volunteer any more, Lambert said icily, 'We should never have known the time of Matthew Upson's death, for a start.'

Charlie Taggart's mind would not work fast enough, when he wanted it to be at its most acute. He said limply, 'I didn't give you the time of Matt Upson's death. How could—'

'No. You gave us the time when you claimed he was last seen, and left us to work out the time of death for ourselves when the body was eventually found. You and your accomplice here.'

Taggart glanced automatically into the face of the woman beside him, framed in its familiar fair hair, and failed to see the warning in it. He was seeing nothing very clearly now. He gathered himself and said with a desperate aggression, 'I told you when I last saw Matt, that was all! In an innocent attempt to help your enquiries, I told you when I had last seen him! God, you must be desperate to be talking like this. I wish I'd never spoken to you, now!'

'I doubt that, Mr Taggart. You spoke to us quite deliberately, in an attempt to lay a false trail. A successful attempt, I have to admit, for a time at least. You knew perfectly well what you were about. Indeed, you had planned the story carefully, with your fellow-killer here. It was necessary, if you were to divert attention from the time when Matthew Upson actually died to a time for which you both had perfectly good alibis.'

Taggart failed to heed the warning pressure on his arm from the woman beside him: perhaps he did not even feel it. 'I don't know what the hell you're talking about! I saw Matt Upson on that Friday afternoon when he disappeared. About half-past three, as I told you. I remember, because I asked him to go for a drink when—'

'You asked him nothing, because he was dead by then. At your hand, Mr Taggart. Shot through the head, in a copse on the western slopes of the Malverns. At around ten o'clock that morning.'

Liz Upson pulled at his wrist more strongly, felt her hand shaken off, and was forced to speak. She said tersely, 'Leave it, Charlie! Let them try to prove it.'

But Taggart would not heed her warning. He was too excited, too threatened, to stop now. 'I wasn't the only one who saw him that afternoon! Jamie Lawson saw him, too. At three forty-five.'

'No, Mr Taggart, he didn't. Jamie Lawson told us he'd seen Upson at that time, because you threatened him or bribed him in some way. But he didn't see him then, did he? He'd have told us the truth soon enough, once we put him under a little pressure. You knew that. That is why he had to die, isn't it? To preserve the fiction that he had seen Upson alive on that Friday afternoon. He agreed to tell us what must have seemed to him a small lie on your behalf, and it cost him his life.'

Liz Taggart spoke urgently, trying to prevent her lover from wandering deeper into this morass. 'Don't say anything, Charlie! They're whistling in the dark. They haven't a scrap of proof!'

Lambert turned his attention to her. Her face was flushed with a desperate defiance. She brushed a strand of blonde hair angrily away from her temple, as if it might distract her from the contest. He said coldly, 'You had some lies of your own for us, hadn't you? Your husband didn't have a licence for the pistol that killed him, because he never held a firearm at all. Either you or Mr Taggart here brought that pistol to the scene of the murder. I doubt that Matthew Upson had ever seen it before it was used to shoot him through the head on that Friday morning. You drove him out to that deserted spot in the Malverns and then one of you shot him cold-bloodedly through the temple.'

It was a hideous attempt at gallantry which finally cracked Taggart's shaken resolve. He blurted out, 'It wasn't Liz! She would never have shot him. I brought the pistol. I was the one who killed him!'

He stopped aghast, breathing heavily in the silence which followed. His attempt to shield her brought no thanks from the woman beside him. Liz Upson did not even glance at him as she hissed through clenched teeth, 'You fool, Charlie! You stupid, blundering fool!'

He looked at her, stunned, as if he could not believe these words were coming from the lips which had muttered so many tendernesses into his ear. Lambert took advantage of his disorder to say, 'And Jamie Lawson had to die, to protect your story of having seen Upson alive that afternoon. He was the only other person who claimed to have seen him alive as late as that. You knew he wouldn't stick to his story, once we were able to press him.'

Taggart spoke with a curious, distant disgust. 'He was useless, that kid. Up to his eyes in heroin, most of the time. We should never have used him. But he was easy, once I agreed I'd support his case to stay on his course.'

'Pity you did. It meant he lost his life at twenty. And all for nothing, in the end.'

'He's no loss to the world. He was selling coke around the campus. The world is better off without the likes of Jamie Lawson.'

For an instant, Taggart's face showed the ruthlessness which underlay the coolly planned murder of Matthew Upson

184

and the callous dispatch of the student who had pushed his drugs on the campus. Lambert said, 'I've no doubt a DNA test will prove your presence in Lawson's room on the night he died. There were fibres from someone else's clothing on the body and hairs from another head upon the chair you rigged for his fall.'

'He was too far gone to resist. Out of his head on coke, the young fool!' muttered Taggart. He appeared to think the boy's weakness meant that he had deserved his fate; Lambert had seen enough murderers to find this suspension of the normal moral code familiar.

At a nod from his superintendent, Hook stepped forward and pronounced the formal words of arrest over the guilty pair. Lambert stayed with them whilst Hook went outside and beckoned Mark Whitwell to drive forward and assist in the transfer of the pair to the cells at Oldford.

Liz Upson had dismissed Charlie Taggart from the moment when he stumbled into confession. She stared straight ahead of her, with a haughty disdain, which might in other circumstances have had something splendid about it.

Bert Hook, coming back from the street outside into that oppressive room, hoped that she might have been looking at the photographs of her children upon the top of the television cabinet. He said quietly, 'I've radioed for a woman police constable. The children will be taken care of, when they come home.'

It seemed to take her a moment to realise that he was speaking to her. She nodded sharply two or three times. 'Will they be taken into care?'

'That's not a police matter. They'll be well looked after.' Bert was glad that he had not seen these two children, not many years younger than his own two boisterous boys. He would not be able to picture their bewildered, anguished faces when he lay awake in the quiet hours of the night.

DC Whitwell had radioed for reinforcements and Taggart was taken away with a policeman on each side of him in the marked police car. His white face looked back briefly at the woman who had killed with him as he was driven away. If she saw him, she did not acknowledge it. She sat beside Hook without saying a word on her journey towards a life sentence.

The steeply rising ridge of the Malverns towered above Lambert as he drove back along the B4232 towards Oldford, passing very near the point where the discovery of Upson's body had set this case in train.

Normally he felt a surge of exultation at the arrest which marked the successful conclusion of a murder hunt. This time there was nothing; nothing but the bleak emptiness of that second death, which might have been prevented if only he had been quicker to see through the cloud of lies which had obfuscated the first.

He knew that it wasn't only his fault, that there were others as well as he who had accepted the murderers' version of events too easily. It was the kind of consolation he had offered often enough to other officers, but couldn't accept for himself. Perhaps, as retirement loomed closer with each passing year, age was affecting the precision of his thinking.

As he turned the old Vauxhall Senator towards home that night, he felt the familiar sharp pain down the left-hand side of his chest. He smiled, as though welcoming an old friend. Only a touch of fibrositis.

HB JF

DEMCO